Billy's Brain Booster Juice

Becci Murray

For Tabitha

ISBN: 978-1-9162069-0-8

Published by Llama House Children's Books

CONTENTS

1

THE RECIPE

I eat my lunch in a corner of the playground. There's a low wall to sit on and three skinny weeds growing up through a crack in the concrete. Behind the wall there's a small patch of mud, where sometimes, during the rainy season, a puddle of water collects on the soil. It's a brilliant time of year, the rainy season. When the rain comes down, the worms come *up!*

We have a lot of fun, the worms and I. I prefer them to the other children and they prefer me to hungry blackbirds. We dig about in the mud and play *Attack of the Space Dinosaur* with a make-shift paper aeroplane. I drew eyes on it with my pencil to make it more life-like.

"BILLY RADCLIFFE!" That was the dinner-lady. She's never happy, especially not when it's raining. "BILLY RADCLIFFE, GET OUT OF THAT MUD AND OVER HERE *PRONTO!*"

Uh oh. I'd been too busy playing with worms to hear the end-of-lunch bell. You see, Curly (he's my best worm friend) had just narrowly escaped the evil clutches of a flying outer-space dinosaur (the Birdasaurus Pex) by diving for cover beneath the head of a dandelion. The paper plane was sent hurtling into the mud nose first, leaving an enormous crater where it landed.

KA-BOOM!

Oh, how we laughed!

"BILLY *RADCLIFFE!*" cried the dinner-lady, her cheeks turning pink. "EVERYONE ELSE HAS LINED UP FOR CLASS, SO *WHAT*, MAY I ASK, MAKES *YOU* SO SPECIAL?!"

"Nothing," I replied miserably, fishing the Birdasaurus Pex out of the puddle (you have to be nice to alien lifeforms in case they take over the world), when…

Wait a minute. What was this in the hole beneath the tail of the plane? Something white was poking out through the soil. There had never been *anything* in the mud before. Well, nothing but rain and worms and the Birdasaurus Pex, that is. But now, before my startled young eyes, as wondrous as a shooting star on a dreary night, lay a fairly soggy, very dirty…*piece of paper!*

Okay, it may not sound like the most exciting thing in the world. But when your friends are all worms and you've spent ten years playing with mud, it's pretty darn great, I can tell you.

"BILLY RADCLIIIIIIIFFE!"

The dinner-lady's face had gone red like a radish. Any redder and her head would go pop like a pimple. Quickly, I grabbed the piece of paper and shoved it into my pocket, then I ran from my corner to join the queue of sniggering faces.

At school we line up like books in a library. You know, A – Z? That puts me between Pamela O'Donnell and Robert Williams.

Marvellous.

Not.

Robert is twice the size of me in both directions and he stamps on my feet as we walk into class. Every day from the back of the line, he whispers a message to Pamela, who whispers it to the boy next to *her*, who whispers it to the girl next to *him* (and so on and so forth), until the whisper has echoed its way to the front of the line, where Dana Aintree screeches it out like a blast on a referee's whistle.

"Billy's *brain's* made of *worm* slime!"

"Billy can't spell his own *name!*"

"Billy takes his *socks* off to count up to *twenty!*"

"Billy's a total *moron!*"

It's true what they say, except for the bit about

the worm slime, which is why the stupid whispering game hurts more than a stamp on the foot.

But today, nothing would get me down. Today, I was much too excited about my damp piece of paper to care about bullies like Dana or Robert. And so, as I reached the cloakroom, I hung my coat on its peg and carefully de-crumpled the page.

"Wha' cha got there, Radcliffe?"

Robert Williams towered over my left shoulder like some thundering great gorilla.

"I, erm, nothing. That is, I, erm…what?"

He snatched the paper out of my hand.

"I wants to know wha' it is, Radcliffe. Ya'd better tell me right now or I'll 'av to thump ya."

"It's, erm, paper, Robert, I think."

"Is that menna be *funny?*" he growled, spit bubbles collecting like frog-spawn at both corners of his mouth. "Are you reckonin' I'm stoopid or wha'?"

"No, of course not, Robert, no. No!"

"Good, coz I en't the stoopid one, Radcliffe. It's you oo's the stooped one. Now, tell me wha' this is or *I'll 'av to thump ya!"*

Dana Aintree and three of her squeaky little friends had gathered around us to watch. They stood behind Robert with their arms sharply folded and thin smirks painted neatly across their perfectly formed faces.

"*That's* not very *nice,* Robert," mewed Dana, shifting her weight at least once every sentence. "I'm sure *Billy's* good at *something.*"

Well, this was weirder than the paper in the mud. Dana Aintree hated me for being so stupid, always had done. She'd stuck a sign on my back once to say so.

"Thanks," I told her. "But I'm not sure that's–"

"*I* know something you're *good* at," she grinned, talking so loudly the whole cloakroom could hear. "I *saw* you last week in *class,* Billy, picking your *nose* with the end of your *pencil.* You were quite good at *that.*" It wasn't true. Honest. I'm terrible at picking my nose with a pencil. "In *fact,*" she went on, her immaculate friends beaming from ear-ring to ear-ring, "if there was some kind of an *award* for nose-picking, like, *I* don't know…"

"The Nose-bel Prize!" squawked one of the girls with delight.

"Yes, very *good,* Mandy – the Nose-bel Prize. If there was an *award* for nose-picking, even the *pickiest* of nose-picker pickers would pick *you,* Billy Radcliffe, as the greatest *picker* of all time."

She must've been ages thinking that one up.

The rest of our class hooted and snorted with

glee. They were always hooting and snorting at something or another, usually me.

Dana whipped the paper out of Robert's fat fingers.

"Let me *see* that," she demanded. I snuck a quick peep at the page. It looked like a list of some sort. "What *is* this, Billy? You'd better tell me right *now,* or I'll *rip* it to *pieces.*"

The cloakroom hushed to a silent stare.

GULP!

"It's, erm, it's..." Say something, Billy. Say something smart, say something clever, say something witty. For crying out loud, Billy, just – say – *something!* "It's a shopping list."

Dana Aintree rolled her eyes.

"I can see it's a *shopping* list. I'm not an *idiot,* you know? What I *mean* is, why is your *shopping* list so *weird?"*

Use your brain, Billy, use your head. Think, Billy, think!

"Well, Mum likes to be in the kitchen," I told her. This much was true. Mum spent all day, every day in the kitchen, playing poker with Mrs Pollychamp from next door. "She gave me that list to buy some ingredients. She's probably baking a cake or something."

Silence.

And then the cloakroom exploded with laughter.

PAHAHAHAHAHAAAAAA!

Dana Aintree crossed her legs and jumped around as if she might wet herself.

PAHAHAHAHAHAAAAAA!

Mandy Langton snorted so hard a snot-bubble came out of her nose.

PAHAHAHAHAHAAAAAA!

And Robert Williams clung onto his stomach, until, with a loud booming noise (one I supposed was meant to mimic an explosion) he threw himself onto the floor, shouting, "Me sides, me sides! Radcliffe, yer so stoopid ya've split me sides!"

PAHAHAHAHAHAAAAAA!

At that moment, the dark shadow of Mrs Granger fell on top of us like the lid had been placed on our coffin. The spare bit of skin that hung from her throat quivered with rage as she seethed her coffee-ridden breath across the cloakroom and into our terrified faces. (Somewhere that breath has formed clouds – it'll be raining Cappuccino as we speak.)

"WHO IS RESPONSIBLE FOR THIS *HAPPINESS*?" she bawled, walloping Joseph Compton with a rolled-up register for no particular reason.

The teacher strode towards us like an angry bear in a pink floral dress.

Dana Aintree thrust the paper back into my hand.

"It's Billy *Radcliffe,* Miss," cooed the girl, her eyelashes fluttering like a couple of hairy butterflies trying to escape the sticky surface of her sickly-sweet face. Her voice made me feel like I'd eaten twelve jars of chocolate spread and a whole pot of jam. "He's being *thick* again, Miss."

"Is – that – so?" growled the teacher, to which I nodded. It was either that or get thumped by Robert Williams. "Then you and your lonely little braincell will spend all afternoon at the Silent Table. I will not tolerate *thickies* in my classroom, Barney No-Brain, so pack it in, right?"

Mrs Granger had called me Barney since my very first day at school and I'd been too scared to correct her ever since. But the 'No-Brain' bit was new.

As we entered the classroom, everyone sat in their usual places. Everyone except *me*. I went to the back of the room and settled down at the Silent Table, far away from the other children's desks, where Mrs Granger isolated her victims like a lion picking deer from a herd. She would separate us from our friends and not let us speak for a whole day, sometimes even a week, and that's why everyone hated the Silent Table.

But me? I *loved* the Silent Table. You see, I had no friends, not really (well, none who wouldn't get eaten by sparrows during mid-morning break). So, to me, the Silent Table meant Robert Williams couldn't stamp on my feet and Dana Aintree couldn't splatter me with her sparkly lip-gloss. Marvellous! Plus, today I would have total privacy in which to inspect my grubby piece of paper.

Quietly and carefully, I took out the page and opened it under the desk:

Mustard
Garlic
Blue Cheese
Baked beans
Celery
Toothpaste
Liver
Pickled eels
Crab-eyes...

Pickled eels and crab eyes?! No wonder the others had laughed when I told them my mum bakes cakes with this stuff. The very thought of it made the spaghetti-hoop sandwich I had eaten for lunch churn faster by the second, so I folded the paper in half and…

That's when I realised it. *That's* when I saw it. Something else was written on the other side of the page, in letters that were big and bold. I tilted my chair and peered down my nose, wobbling dangerously on two plastic chair-legs.

It wasn't a shopping list. It was a recipe. A recipe for…

Auntie Brenda's Brain Booster Juice

Well, that was about as much excitement as my spaghetti-hoop sandwich could take. The little orange circles leapt from my stomach and squirted most *un*-silently all over the freshly-polished surface of the Silent Table, as I and my now even soggier piece of paper toppled backwards off the chair.

2

CRAB-EYES AND PICKLED EELS

Everyone was thrilled at my vomitus display. Even the terrible Mrs Granger smirked from behind her English Writing Skills Handbook before shoving a mint imperial in her mouth to stifle her laughter.

"Barney No-Brain," she sniggered, "how *dare* you brighten my beige carpet with the orange contents of your stomach? Fetch a mop and bucket from the caretaker's cupboard and clean it up sharpish. Oh, and Barney…"

"Yes, Mrs Granger?"

"Try to find half a brain-cell in there while you're at it. Spaghetti hoop sandwiches, indeed. What a weirdo."

Dana Aintree splattered me with lip-gloss as I walked past her desk.

"Nicely done, Billy Rad*sick*," she sneered, kicking me hard on the shin. "Been eating your mother's *cakes*, have you?"

Hardy-ha-ha, Dana.

The caretaker's cupboard was at the far end of the main corridor. We weren't allowed to keep buckets in the classrooms anymore. Buckets had been banned since Robert Williams was caught hatching alligator-eggs in one. He had stored it behind a cushion in the library, until, one day, the creatures grew big enough to climb *out* of the bucket and roam around the school at will. The headmaster mistook one young reptilian for a three-hole-punch, stuffed a wad of paper in its mouth and bashed the poor thing on the head. It took three operations to sew the finger back on and one kind zoo keeper to take the frightened beast back to where it belonged (the alligator, that is, not the headmaster). It was a shame really - it would've made a terrific Birdasaurus Pex (again, the alligator, not the headmaster).

When I reached the cupboard, I snuck another look at the recipe. Auntie Brenda's Brain Booster Juice – what a thought! And who needed their brain boosting more than me? No-one, that's who. How wonderful it would be to come into school the following day with a brain the size of Venus. Everybody would be *so* jealous, especially that horrible Dana Aintree and her gaggle of tag-along friends.

There was just one problem. Where was I going to get hold of all these strange ingredients? You can't just pop to the supermarket and buy crab-eyes you know, and never in my life had I seen pickled eels at the corner shop. No, I needed someone with special contacts in the world of fishmongering, someone like…someone like…

"Colin Bradley!"

As if by magic, Colin Bradley appeared at the other end of the corridor, a dustpan in one hand and a brush in the other.

He looked terrified at the sound of his name.

"Are you going to hit me?" he asked. "Only, I'm armed, you know," and he waved the plastic brush like a sword.

"No, Colin, it's me, Billy. Billy Radcliffe. I'm in the year below you. We sat at the Hopeless-Case Table together during Maths Week last year, remember?"

"Oh yeah, that's right," he said, lowering the brush. "You had lip-gloss in your hair." He peered up at my head. "You've *still* got lip-gloss in your hair."

Colin Bradley is the only other child at my school who's as bullied as me. He's not very clever and he reeks of fish, so the other children are awful to him.

We're quite similar, I suppose, except I don't smell and Colin doesn't have his own worms in a corner of the playground. Instead, he walks around the edge of the netball court, humming to himself in more ways than one.

"What's with the dustpan, Colin?" I asked.

The boy sighed. "I broke the electric pencil sharpener. The shavings went all over the book corner carpet. Mr Sampson says I'm to clear it up and then I'm to save my pocket money until I can buy him a new one. He reckons I'll be thirty-seven by the time I can afford it." He pointed to the orange stain on my shirt. "Are you saving that spaghetti hoop for later, Billy?"

"No, I was sick on the Silent Table," I explained.

"Oh dear. Sad times."

"Yeah, sad times. Listen, Colin, your dad's a fishmonger, isn't he?"

"That's right. He's got a stall near the sea-front. I'm going to work there when I leave school. Fish don't care how well you can read. Especially not once they're filleted."

"Cool." There was a moment's silence where we both realised I wasn't cool enough to say 'cool'. "What types of fish does he sell?"

"Oh, all sorts. Cod, bass, plaice, turbot, brill,

pollock, mackerel, herring..."

I sensed this could go on for a while.

"How about pickled eels and crab-eyes?" I cut in.

Colin frowned with suspicion.

"Pickled eels and crab-eyes?"

"They're for a recipe I'm trying out. Crab-eye soup with pickled eel croutons. It's, erm, Japanese."

"Oh my *cod!*" cried the smelly boy, his face lighting up like a giant supernova. "I *love* crab-eye soup with pickled eel croutons! Do you want a jellyfish?"

I didn't know what to say. No-one had ever thought I wanted a jellyfish before.

"Well, that's all right, thanks, Colin. I'm not a big fan of jelly."

"No, me neither. Dad likes to dip one in his crab-eye soup, but it's a bit weird, if you ask me. Look, I'd better get back to class now. I'll bring your stuff into school tomorrow. See you then, Billy," and he disappeared down the corridor in a haze of fishiness.

The next morning, I arrived at school to find Colin Bradley waiting in my corner of the playground, a paper bag in one hand and a jam-jar in the other.

"The crab-eyes are in here," he said, passing me

the bag. Inside the jar there were a dozen or so slimy, black creatures pressing against the glass. "And those are the eels."

"They look like slugs," I grimaced, handing him the money. "What do they taste like?"

"Fish," he said cheerily, as if this was a good enough explanation. "Dad ate an electric eel once. Mum was surprised he didn't electrocute himself, but Dad was more *shocked* than anyone."

Suddenly, Colin started making an awful honking sound, like a seagull with a party blower lodged in its gullet. He honked and he honked and he wouldn't stop, over and over again, until the whole school were staring and pointing at both of us. At first, I thought he was choking. Then I wondered if he was doing an impression of his dad being electrocuted by an eel.

"SHOCKED!" shrieked the smelly boy. "MY DAD ATE AN ELECTRIC EEL AND THEN HE WAS *SHOCKED!* DO YOU GET IT, BILLY, DO YOU GET IT?!"

I didn't get it. The only thing I'd ever got was chicken-pox.

"That's great, Colin," I said. "Really funny."

"I knew you'd like that one, Billy," smiled Colin, once he'd finally calmed down. "We're peas in a pod, me and you. Anyway, enjoy your soup. If you need anything else, just ask," and he started his sixteen laps of the netball court, chewing on a pink sea-stick and humming an old sea shanty as he went.

The rest of my day was spent counting down the seconds until home-time, so that when the final bell sounded I could shoot from that school like an outer-space dinosaur through a blackhole, all the way to The Next-Door Shop with my recipe.

The door went *TING!* as I opened it. There was a poster sticky-tacked to the glass. On it was a picture of a boy holding a carton of…

"HARPING'S ORANGE DRINK," said the poster. **"START YOUR DAY WITH A GLASS OF FRESHLY-MADE *JUICE!*"**

The word 'Juice' made my spine tingle, as if someone had just dropped a slimy pickled eel down the back of my shirt.

"I will," I replied, "but it won't be freshly-made *orange* juice – it'll be freshly-made *Brain Booster* Juice," and I blitzed the aisles in a rapturous whirl of ingredients, until every penny of my pocket money had been spent.

The Next-Door Shop was next-door to my house, which is why we call it The Next-Door Shop (everyone else just calls it The Shop), so I was home in no time with four carrier bags of goodies. Mum was in the kitchen, as usual, playing poker with Mrs Pollychamp. I apologised for disturbing their game, grabbed a plastic bowl and a big wooden spoon, and then did three hard blinks at my mum before heading upstairs (this let her know Mrs Pollychamp had three-of-a-kind and made sure I'd get more pocket money the following day).

GERRR-SPLAT!

A zombie exploded as I reached the landing. The sound of it came from the room next to mine and it meant three things: 1) my big brother wasn't at school (again), 2) Mum hadn't noticed he wasn't at school (again), and 3) he would be on his computer until midnight because tomorrow he wouldn't go to school (again), all of which made sure I could make my marvellous Brain Booster Juice without being questioned.

With trembling hands, I laid the ingredients out on the bed. They looked like the world's worst picnic and my stomach screamed at the sight of them.

"Save me!" it begged, and, *"Don't do it!'* it wailed, but I emptied all the packets, tins and tubes into the bowl, picked up the spoon and...

What now? There were no instructions about

how to make the Juice, just a list of ingredients. Should I fry it, poach it, boil it or toast it? Should I bake it like a pie, or simmer it like an egg?

"Auntie Brenda's Brain Booster Juice," I read from the page, remembering the poster from The Next-Door Shop. "Brain Booster *Juice*. It doesn't need cooking at all – it needs juicing!"

Of course, you can't *juice* a tube of toothpaste or a tin of baked beans, so I did the next best thing, and stirred. I stirred and I stirred, until the mixture looked smoother and runnier. And when I had stirred for an hour, I stirred it some more, and then more, until my aching arm threatened to drop from my body and the stench of all those yucky ingredients filled my bedroom like a fart in a tea-cup. It was a horrible, sticky kind of a smell, one that seeped through my clothes and into my skin, until every part of my body could taste the pong.

Think about flowers, I told myself, trying not to gag as the spoon turned the mixture, *think about ripe peaches and fields of freshly mown grass.*

But the flowers had died, the peaches were mouldy and the grass was covered in cow-pats (big runny ones with steam coming off them), so I darted out of my bedroom, gasping the clean air like medicine.

"A longer handle," I panted. "I need a longer handle so I can mix the Juice from further away," and strangely enough, all that lovely Brain Booster stink must've done me some good, because this, it turned out, was a *great* plan.

I forged my invention from a packet of rolled up playing cards (Mum's old ones, of course), which I carefully joined together with sticky tape to form a long and hollow sort of pole, before attaching the wooden spoon to its end. I called it my Brain Booster Juicer and it worked brilliantly, so ten minutes later the Juice was down in the hallway and *I* was upstairs on the landing, stirring the mixture with an extra-large clothes peg attached to my nose.

Before long my concoction looked like a tub of melted ice-cream with the odd raisin or two floating about in the froth (the crab-eyes didn't blend in), and there it was – *my very first batch of Auntie Brenda's Brain Booster Juice!*

Carefully, I poured the mixture into an empty fizzy-drink bottle and screwed on the cap.

"I'll drink you in the morning," I whispered, "first thing in the morning. And then I, stupid Barney No-Brain, will be the cleverest child in the whole school."

Marvellous!

3

THE FIRST BATCH

I wanted to drink the Juice as close to school time as possible, so I waited until I was almost ready to leave the house before unscrewing the lid. The smell hit me like a slap on the face and I knew it would taste even worse. If I had a straw, I could direct the mixture straight down my throat and save myself the horror of all those awful ingredients sloshing around in my mouth.

With no time to lose, I rummaged through my bedside cabinet. There were thwarted space dinosaurs and conkers and cars, and several mouldy sandwich crusts, the likes of which you could crack walnuts with. And there, at the very back was a long, white, curly straw I'd got free with a chicken nugget meal last summer – I'd known it was in there somewhere.

"Well, here goes nothing," I said, closing my eyes and placing the straw to my lips.

And I sucked.

GLUG, GLUG, GLUG, GLUG…

The mixture was thick and gummy, and it glooped from the end of the straw like tar, sliding over my tongue and coating my taste-buds like glue. It tasted exactly the same as it smelt, only stronger and with a hint of cheesy yuckiness. Then a crab-eye got stuck in the straw. I had to suck hard to dislodge it and the horrible thing slammed into the back of my throat with a fishy explosion, the likes of which you could never imagine, not even in your very worst nightmares.

But I was determined, and I gulped down those heavy globs of eyebally Brain Booster until my gargling stomach felt fit to burst and the bottle was almost half empty – I would save the rest for tomorrow.

"Billy!" called a voice from downstairs. "Get down here! I've fried you a kipper for breakfast!"

A long, fishy burp blasted out of my mouth.

"Thanks, Mum," I replied, somehow managing to keep down the Brain Booster despite the smell of kippers. "But I might have some toast instead."

Robert Williams made sicky noises in my ear as we headed into the cloakroom that morning.

"Are ya gunna puke again today, Radcliffe? Are you gunna chuck up on Mrs Gee's table like ya did yesterday?"

Dana Aintree cackled like a witch.

"Yeah, *Billy,* does the thought of runny *eggs* and *nose* slime make you want to go *blargh?*" Nose slime? Who calls it nose slime? "Or how about mouldy *cheese* and *feet*-sweat? Or crunchy *raisins* and *mouse* poo? Or something even *weirder* like *spaghetti hoop sandwiches!*"

Dana's clones hugged each other and chirruped loudly.

"I'm okay, thanks, Dana," I told her, staring the hateful girl square in the eye. "But having to look at *your face* might do it."

Silence.

And then, what on earth had just happened? Had I *actually* said something clever?

Of course, Robert immediately hung me from a coat hook by the back of my jumper, but I didn't care. I swung proudly on my peg for a full twenty-five minutes, until Mrs Granger finally noticed my absence from class and hit me with an electric fly-swat until I dropped to the floor.

"Right then, listen up, you lot," the teacher began, as I took my usual place next to Joseph Compton at the Wally Table, "it's maths quiz time. As always, the team to answer the most questions correctly will get to choose this week's class book. And if anyone else chooses that namby-pamby wishy-washy ballet tripe, I shall read 'War and Peace' again...backwards!"

Dana and her weasel-like pals from the Vaguely Clever Table had won the maths quiz for the last twelve weeks, so the rest of us had suffered an entire series about a ballerina named Angel Twinkletoes. Nobody liked the stupid ballerina stories except Dana. In fact, Joseph Compton had fallen asleep in the middle of the first book. He still has the scar from where his face hit the corner of the desk.

As for me, I'd got my eye on a brilliant book about an intergalactic, fire-breathing dragon. It had been on display in the rack above the bookcase for months now and the picture on the cover looked a lot like the Birdasaurus Pex.

But we would never win. You see, our table consisted of me, Joseph Compton, David Duhbrain, Nicola Nosenowt and Felicity Finkslow (obviously not their real names, but you get the picture). Last week, Joseph Compton told Mrs Granger that a times-table was, "A desk you can tell the time with, Miss," and as a punishment for being so stupid, she stapled him to a display board by the back of his shirt.

He dangled there for almost an hour.

"First question," began the teacher, sipping her mug of black coffee with a horrible slurp. "What is 74 add 12?"

Dana Aintree's hand shot into the air like a rocket, her lips pressed firmly together as if stuck tight with super-glue.

"You there," said Mrs Granger, peering over her spectacles, "Dana What's-Your-Face."

"74 add 12 is *86*, Mrs Granger."

"Correct." The teacher wrote a small number one on the white-board next to Dana's team's name, 'The Ballet Beauties', who each high-fived Dana in turn. "Next question. What is 15 minus 4?"

A voice came from the back of the room.

"11, Mrs Granger," it said.

Everyone swivelled around on their chairs, wondering who had answered the question. But Mrs Granger was staring at the Wally Table as if trying to focus on something a really long way in the distance.

And then she looked a bit put out.

"Barney No-Brain, how *dare* you speak without raising your hand?"

"What? But I—"

"One point *off* 'The Astronaut Chums'."

"Ya mean, 'Astronaut *Bums*'!" laughed Robert, and the rest of the class roared with laughter.

"Enough with the *HAPPY FACES!*" bawled Mrs Granger. "The Wally Table have minus one point. What a surprise. Now, where did I put my stapler?"

That was odd. Mrs Granger seemed to think it was *me* who had answered that question. But I'd never answered a question before in my life. Well, not without being stapled to a display board afterwards.

"The next question is difficult," said the teacher, "so *think* before shouting out something random and fluking upon the answer," and she shot me a look as if to say, "That means *you*, Barney No-Brain," before turning back to her notes. "What is 15 multiplied by 3?"

The Vaguely Clever Table started to work out the sum on a piece of rough paper.

SCRIBBLE, SCRIBBLE, SCRIBBLE…

But then they put down their pens and turned slowly, glaring at me like a pack of space dinosaurs hunting a lone worm. What had I done *now?*

"Barney No-Brain," snapped Mrs Granger, "stop interrupting my maths quiz. If you need the toilet, just go."

Seeing my confusion, Joseph Compton pointed to the space above my head. I looked up, and there, to my horror, *was my hand!* Yes, there was my arm, as straight and as tall as a washing line pole, as stiff as the hair on Mrs Granger's chin, and there was my hand on the end of it, waving around like it knew how to answer the question.

A surge of panic rushed over me. I didn't know what 15 multiplied by 3 was.

"I don't need the toilet, Mrs Granger," I replied.

"All the more reason to stop interrupting my maths quiz then," snapped the teacher. "Unless... You're not going to vomit again, are you? Barney No-Brain, if you throw up in my maths quiz, it'll be the *last* thing you do."

One of Dana's friends began giggling in sparrow-like twitters.

"He thinks he knows the answer, Mrs Granger. *That's* why Billy's raised his hand – he thinks he knows the answer to the question!"

Robert Williams thumped the table and boomed with laughter, as Dana Aintree's face rippled with joy.

Silently, the teacher removed her glasses and placed them down on the desk. It was always worse when Mrs Granger looked at you without her glasses on. Every blink was like a karate chop to your stomach.

"This should be good," sneered the teacher.

"Come on then, Barney, astound us. What is 15 multiplied by 3?"

"It's…it's…" I could hardly hear my own voice over the thump of my racing heart. "It's 45, Mrs Granger."

GASP!

That was the whole class taking one giant breath of surprise, a giant breath that fluttered Mrs Granger's chin-skin like a flag.

And that's when I realised *the Juice was working!*

Mrs Granger showed no reaction at all to my sudden outburst of cleverness. In fact, she barely even blinked. She just sat there, emotionless, her large black stapler poised dangerously close to her face, until suddenly slamming it down on the desk and smashing her glasses to pieces.

"Barney No-Brain," she seethed, through her stained teeth, "you owe me a new pair of spectacles. One point to the 'Astronaut Chums'."

Joseph Compton patted me on the back, shaking his head in disbelief but smiling widely, as Dana Aintree rounded on me like I'd just kicked someone's puppy.

"Don't you *dare* put your hand up *again*, Billy Radcliffe," she spat, "do you *hear* me? If you put your hand up *again*, Billy Radcliffe, you'll be *sorry*, got it?"

before turning back to her team-mates.

'The Ballet Beauties' sat eagerly in their seats as Mrs Granger began the next question, their necks tall like meercats, their ears pricked like rabbits, their eye-lids batting like, well, bats, I suppose.

"If Arjun has 20 eggs, and he gives 3 eggs to Sarah and 4 to David, how many eggs does he–"

My hand was already up. I didn't want it to be up, it just went on its own, as if someone had pulled at its string.

Mrs Granger squinted blindly at it from across the classroom.

"Barney?" she asked, checking the hand did in fact belong to me.

"Yes, Mrs Granger," I replied. "I'm over here, at the back. And the answer is 13 eggs."

I hadn't worked it out. I *couldn't* work it out. It just felt like the right thing to say.

And by the look on Mrs Granger's face, it *was* the right thing to say.

"He's *cheating,*" whined Dana, jumping out of her chair with disgust. "Billy Radcliffe has *stolen* your *questions,* Mrs Granger, and looked up the *answers.* It's not *fair,* Miss, it's not *fair!*"

Mrs Granger pieced her glasses back together with a strip of masking tape and a lump of sticky-tack. Then she picked up her stapler and stroked it like a shiny black cat.

"Of course he's cheating, Dana What's-Your-Face. But what to do about it…what to do…?"

PING!

An absentminded staple shot across the classroom, narrowly missing Joseph Compton's shoulder and hammering itself into the back of his chair.

"I've got it!" Mrs Granger cried suddenly, with an unusually cheerful expression. It was the first time she'd smiled without someone having broken a leg or cracked their head open. "We'll have a spelling bee! I've been planning a good spelling bee for *years*. Here's what you do: everyone lines up at the front of the room and I give each of you a word to spell out loud. Spell it correctly, and you remain standing. Spell it wrongly, and you're out of the game. It's going to be so much fun, and, more to the point, no-one will be able to *cheat,* Barney No-Brain, because nobody knows about my Special Spelling Bee Folder, so, nah!"

PING!

A second staple shot past Joseph's ear, hit the sink on the far wall and bounced around the room like popcorn in a microwave.

It was time for the spelling bee to begin.

As the class lined up, Mrs Granger took her Special Spelling Bee Folder from her desk drawer. It didn't look very special. Okay, so she'd covered it with tin-foil and written 'Special Spelling Bee Folder' on it with a marker pen, but that was as special as it got.

Dana Aintree was the first in the line, partly because her name was at the top of the register but mostly because she shoved Jessica Murphy from the front of the queue with her bony little elbows.

"Dana What's-Your-Face, spell – 'dog," Mrs Granger instructed, with a silly open-mouthed grin, "as in, my dog is a Yorkshire Terrier."

"That's *easy*, Mrs Granger. D – O – G, *dog*."

"Very good!" whooped the teacher, with a small bounce in her chair. "Okay, the next word is for you, Michael Thingamy."

As she moved along the row, Mrs Granger ticked off the words in her folder until finally reaching those of us at the other end of the line. It was my turn next. The teacher curled her top lip when she saw me, as if she had just smelt something she'd done in a teacup.

"Ugh," she said, "it's *you*. Barney, spell – 'ant', as in, my brain is the size of an ant."

"A – N – T, ant," I said, clearly.

"Give the boy a sticker," mocked Mrs Granger. "I've known goldfish who can spell 'ant'. Your turn next, Katie Doo-Dah…"

Of course, the words got harder as the game went on, much like the crusts in my bedside cabinet, and although everyone got their first word right, by the ninth word only four of us remained: Dana Aintree, Mandy Langton, Peter Giselle and myself.

"Round *nine!*" whooped Mrs Granger, now hopping from one foot to the other as she turned the next page of her Special Spelling Bee Folder. "Dana, spell – 'sausage,' as in, I like sausage and chips for my tea."

Dana spelled the word correctly and then shot me a conceited look as the rest of the class cheered loudly. Then Mandy Langton's word was 'luxury', into which she added an extra 'r', before Peter Giselle spelled his word 'celery' wrongly by starting it with the letter 's'.

I was next.

"Barney No-Brain," began Mrs Granger, "if you spell the next word correctly, you will be in the final round against Dana What's-Your-Face." Dana threw a flower-shaped rubber at my head. "Spell it wrongly, and Dana wins. Got it?"

Remarkably, I *did* get it. And I hadn't even been

listening.

"Okay, Barney, spell – 'rhododendron'."

"What?!"

"As in, I cannot spell the word 'rhododendron'."

"But that's not fair, Mrs Granger! She gets to spell 'sausage' and I have to spell 'rhododendron'?"

"SILENCE!" roared the teacher, and the whole world obeyed. "I'm warning you, Barney, there's a display board in that corridor with your name written all over it. 'Rhododendron' is the next word in my folder, so *that* is the word you will spell. Or *not* spell, as the case may be."

Everyone in the room knew she was lying. They knew she couldn't bear the thought of me, stupid Billy Radcliffe, going into the spelling bee final with Dana Aintree.

"But, Mrs Granger," I said, "I don't even know what a R-H-O-D-O-D-E-N-D-R-O-N, rhododendron is."

Crikey!

Everyone looked expectantly at Mrs Granger (they didn't know what a rhododendron was either, let alone how to spell it), and the teacher gave them her answer by slumping back in her seat and folding her arms in a huff.

"You've ruined my spelling bee, Barney No-

Brain. I've been working on that for years," and she slammed closed her folder before tossing it into the bin. "Barney's in the last round with Dana. Oh, deep joy. Let's get on with it before the excitement kills me. Dana What's-Your-Face, spell 'antique'. Or don't. I really couldn't care less."

"*Antique,* Mrs Granger? *Antique,* as in…?"

"Antique, as in, stop asking stupid questions and spell it before I staple you up by the *PONY-TAIL!*"

"Got it," replied Dana. "A – N – T – E – E – K, antique."

Mrs Granger made a noise like a gameshow buzzer.

"Uh-uhhh! Wrong! Completely wrong! Stupid girl."

"Are you *sure,* Mrs Granger. I'm not *usually—*"

"Barney, spell 'synonym' and make it snappy. I need a black coffee. Three sugars. Four, possibly."

"S – Y – N – O – N – Y – M, synonym," I said, as loudly and as quickly as possible. "Is that right, Mrs Granger?"

"You know it's right, you nasty little show-off. Barney wins. Whoop-di-flippin'-doo. Now clear off and play in the road while I hang out the bunting. *CLASS DISMISSED!*"

"But, Mrs *Granger,*" whined Dana, burying her

face in her hands, "he can't *win*, he's…well, he's *Billy*, Miss!"

Everyone from the Wally Table congratulated me as we left the classroom that day and later on Mrs Granger read the first chapter of the intergalactic dragon book.

Marvellous!

But do you know what was even better than the laser-shooting space ranger and the terrible outer-space dragon? The thought that tomorrow my brain would be even more boosted when I drank the rest of the Juice.

4

YAAARGH!

At school the next day I found Mrs Granger rooted outside our classroom like an ancient oak tree. I had polished off the second half of the Brain Booster Juice earlier that morning and was still trying to keep it down when the teacher slammed her thick arm across the frame, breathing me in through her cavernous nostrils like a gnat up a couple of drainpipes.

"Not so fast, Barney No-Brain," she sneered. "I've told the headmaster about your smart-alec ways and it's been decided – *you're going up a year,*" and she pointed across the corridor with a fiendish grin.

Oh no, not Mr Sampson's class!

"But, Mrs Granger, I'm not old enough to be in Year 6. Are you sure the headmaster's agreed to it?"

She moulded herself to the shape of the doorway like putty, her eyes sticking out like two pickled onions on sticks.

She certainly *looked* pretty sure.

Well, this was terrible news. Mr Sampson was the weirdest teacher in the whole school. In fact, Mr Sampson was the weirdest teacher in *any* school. He had been a Sea Cadet as a child but was thrown out for being too gung-ho about the whole thing. Some said the sea air must've gone to his head, some said he'd had a nasty run-in with a cuttlefish bone. Whatever the reason, Mr Sampson was less stable than a newborn pony on a loose tightrope.

"Welcome to Year 6, Billy," said the teacher, as I entered the classroom. "Why don't you – HANG THE SCURVY STOWAWAY FROM THE YARDARM! – take a seat next to Colin?"

Colin Bradley beamed like I was the first person who had ever agreed to sit next to him, because, well, I *was* the first person who had ever agreed to sit next to him.

"Wotcha, Billy," he grinned. There was a fish bone stuck between his two front teeth. "Did you have enough crab-eyes for your soup last night?"

The other children on our table went *EWWWW!* and moved their chairs to the other side of the desk. Then one of them sprayed us with a big bottle of perfume, which mixed with the smell of Colin to make one giant stink.

"Okay, class," began Mr Sampson, lifting his

eye-patch in order to see his text book properly, "this morning, we're going to – BEAT THE NASTY BILGE RAT WITH ME PEGLEG! – learn a little bit about science. On each of your tables, you'll find a clear object shaped like the roof of a house."

"They're prisms," I muttered to Colin.

The teacher looked up from his book.

"Sorry, Billy, did you – THIEVE ME LAST DROP O' RUM, YE MANGY SON OF A SEA-DOG! – say something?"

"Yes, sir, I think these house roof shapes are called prisms."

"That's right, Billy. You can take two – PIECES OF EIGHT! PIECES OF EIGHT! – house-points for that." Mr Sampson forced a smile, but the little vein on the side of his head pulsed with a life of its own. "Okay, back to our experiment. I'd like each of you to hold one of the glass shapes up to the window and—"

"They're acrylic," I muttered to Colin.

Mr Sampson calmly placed a fuse into his small desk-top cannon.

"Billy, anyone who wishes to speak during class must first raise their hand. If you don't, I'll have to – FEED YER BONES TO THE FISHES! – take back those house-points, I'm afraid."

"Yes, sir, sorry. It's just, the prisms aren't made of glass, sir. They're acrylic. Acrylic is a type of plastic, sir. It's half the weight of glass and it's impact resistant. Another type of plastic is polyvinyl chloride, more commonly known as PVC."

"Very informative, Billy. You're quite the – SCALLYWAG! LANDLUBBER! SCOUNDREL! – scientist, aren't you? But we really must get on with our work now, so if you don't mind—"

"PVC plastic comes in two forms, sir, flexible and rigid. Rigid PVC is used for items such as bottles and bank cards, whereas flexible PVC is used in the manufacturing of inflatable objects, like that parrot you've got on your shoulder, sir."

What was happening to me? Why couldn't I stop talking about plastic?

"HORNSWAGGLING BARREL-BELLIED BLIGHTER!" cried Mr Sampson.

"PVC was created in 1872 by a German chemist named Eugen Baumann, through the polymerisation of vinyl chloride. Vinyl chloride is an organochloride with the formula $H_2C{=}CHCl$ and is also known as chloroethene, which is produced by the hydrochlorination of–"

"YAAAAARRRRGH!"

Without warning (well, without any *sensible*

warning), Mr Sampson struck a match on his desk, lit the fuse to his desk-top cannon and…

BOOF!

A lukewarm jacket potato hit me in the middle of my forehead.

Colin cringed apologetically, as if to say, "Probably should've warned you about the spud-cannon," before wiping the bits from my face with a crunchy tissue he'd found up his sleeve. Then Mr Sampson swigged at his rum (which was really a bottle of orange squash with *Rum* written on the label), whilst the rest of us got on with the experiment.

"Okay, class, who wants to – DIG FER BURIED TREASURE! – tell us what they saw when the sunlight passed through the shape?" asked the teacher, once we'd all finished holding our prisms up to the window.

A girl at the front raised her hand.

"There were lots of *colours*, Mr Sampson," she said. "They looked a bit like a *rainbow*."

"It's called refraction," I muttered to Colin.

Seriously, why couldn't I just shut up?

The girl called Sally lashed her head around so fast she almost fell off her chair.

"What are you on about *now?*" she spat, her face

so close to mine I could smell the cherry lip-gloss on her breath. "Dana's told me what a *cheater* you are, Billy *Sad*cliffe, so be *quiet* and stop showing *off!*"

Oh good, a new class and a new nickname.

"Refraction," I told her, "is the term used for when light bends, Sally."

"Don't be *ridiculous*. Everyone knows you can't *bend* light, you *idiot*."

The rest of Sally's table swung their blindingly glossy hair from one shoulder to the other and snorted their agreement. They looked like something from a very expensive shampoo advert for pigs.

"Actually, light *can* bend, Sally," I explained. "But the level of refraction is dependent upon the wavelength of the light, so different colours are bent at different angles, thus splitting the original white sunlight into the spectrum you witnessed when you held up the prism." The Sally girl's nostrils flared like a couple of wind-socks. "But well done for spotting the rainbow," I added. "Pretty, was it?"

Mr Sampson's hand was again hovering over his spud-cannon.

"Billy Radcliffe, how do you know so much about today's topic? Mrs Granger thinks you've – PILFERED ME TREASURE MAP, YE MANGY VARMINT! – been stealing the teachers' text books and memorising the answers."

"I didn't steal your text book, sir. It was Isaac Newton, sir."

The teacher scratched at his head.

"Isaac Newton stole my text book?"

"No, sir, Isaac Newton discovered the phenomenon of light dispersion some three-hundred years ago, *that's* how I know about refraction. Isaac Newton and I aren't related, sir, but my family's genealogy *does* run through the line of New*ports*, so the two names may have become intertwined over the years due to–"

"YAAAAAAAARRRGH!"

And then…

BOOF!

Colin pulled another tissue out of his sleeve. There was a bit of prawn stuck to this one.

"Okay, class," said Mr Sampson, the little vein on his head now bulging like a wrestler's bicep, "I want everyone to read quietly whilst I take Billy Radcliffe down to – DAVY JONES'S LOCKER! – see Mr Merriford," and with that, he frog-marched me out of the classroom and towards the headmaster's office.

5

THE HEADMASTER

We found the headmaster hard at work in his office, but when Mr Sampson burst in waving his cutlass (actually a ruler) he put down his crossword puzzle book and smiled keenly.

"Mr Sampson. What brings you here?"

"There's a problem with this – NASTY SON OF A BISCUIT EATER! – new Year 6 boy, I'm afraid, Mr Merriford."

"Problem, Mr Sampson? What sort of a problem?"

"Well, he's caused a bit of – A MUTINY ON THE POOP DECK! – trouble during a science experiment. You see, he already knows everything, sir."

The headmaster laughed heartily.

"Oh, come now, Mr Sampson, that's impossible. Nobody knows *everything*."

"It's true, sir. Mrs Granger thinks so as well. He's a – SWASHBUCKLING BARNACLE-BRAIN! – right little know-it-all, sir."

Mr Merriford came around to the front of the desk and patted my head like a dog. Then he crouched on the floor so his eyes were level with mine, placed his hand on my shoulder and spoke to me as if I was three years old.

"And what about *you*, Billy? Do *you* think you know everything?"

"I…I'm not sure, sir."

"There you go then!" the headmaster exclaimed with triumph. "If the boy doesn't know whether he knows everything or not, then he *doesn't* know everything at all – problem solved, Mr Sampson."

"I'm serious, Mr Merriford," the teacher replied. "This is no – YO HO HO! – laughing matter. Billy Radcliffe *knows everything*."

"I'll tell you what, Mr Sampson, in order to put your mind at rest, I shall ask Billy a series of five questions. When he doesn't know the answers to all of them, it'll prove he doesn't know everything and then he can go back to class. How does that sound, Billy?"

"It sounds…okay, sir," I said.

Mr Merriford chortled.

"Don't look so worried, Billy, it's not a test. It's just an exercise to prove a point. Trust me, you won't know the answers to *any* of the questions *I* have in mind. In fact, if Mr Sampson is right and you answer all five correctly, well, you can jolly well have my job. What do you say to *that* then, Billy?"

"I...I'm not really sure I should say anything, sir."

"Erm, Mr Merriford..." began Mr Sampson.

"Super!" cheered the headmaster, with a clap of his hands. "Let's get cracking then, shall we?" The poor man. He had no idea he was about to go up against Auntie Brenda's Brain Booster Juice. "Okay, Billy, here's your first question – what is the capital of Nepal?" and he raised his eyebrows at Mr Sampson. "I spent a year in Nepal before starting University. Beautiful country, truly lovely. I had a little apartment just west of—"

"Kathmandu."

The headmaster frowned.

"Oh," he said, both surprised and impressed by my answer. "Bit of a geography whiz, are we? Well, good for you, Billy. Let's try some history instead – in 1936, the assassination of which political figure is said to have caused the outbreak of the Spanish Civil War?" Again, he turned to Mr Sampson. "When I left Nepal, I studied Spanish History at Edinburgh University. Fascinating subject, completely enthralling. In our third year, we learnt all about—"

"The assassination of José Calvo Sotelo."

This time, Mr Merriford looked a bit more than surprised. But not quite so impressed.

"How did you—? Right, let's go for a maths question – everyone hates maths, don't they? What is, I don't know, 13,983 divided by 12?"

Snatching a calculator from his desk, the headmaster started tapping at its buttons with the end of a pencil.

"1165.25, sir," I replied. He was still tapping. "Sir, you don't need to do that. It's definitely 1165.25."

He pressed the equals sign and stared at the screen, shaking his head in bewilderment.

"I don't believe it. You've answered three out of five questions correctly. That's—"

"60%, sir."

"I was going to say 'remarkable', but, yes, 60% is about right, Billy."

"It's exactly right, sir."

Mr Sampson gave the headmaster a look as if to say, "Told you so," and a bead of sweat rolled down Mr Merriford's nose. But then he seemed to have an idea.

"Right, no more Mr Nice-Guy," he teased. "Time to bring out the big guns."

Behind the headmaster's desk was a huge cabinet, packed solid with books about every subject you could ever imagine. There were books about cars and space, and some about things I had never heard of before, like horticulture and calligraphy, and there, on the far left-hand side, was a pink book with a picture of a dancer on the spine.

Oh no, not the namby-pamby, wishy-washy ballet tripe!

"Aha – just the ticket!" exclaimed Mr Merriford, taking it down from the shelf.

"Sir, you really mustn't ask me anything about the Angel Twinkletoes books, it wouldn't be fair. Mrs Granger has just read the entire series to our class."

"Yes, but she didn't read *this* one, Billy. *This* one is a brand-new proof copy of the latest book in the series. It's called *Angel Twinkletoes Twirls Around a Bit* and it won't be in book shops for another six months."

"How come *you* have a copy then, sir?"

The headmaster looked sheepish. *So* sheepish he almost went…

BAAAAAAAAAAA!

"Never you mind," he said, placing the book between the palms of his hands and letting it flop open at whichever page it liked. "Okay, here is your fourth question, Billy – on page 78 of *Angel Twinkletoes Twirls Around a Bit,* what does Angel buy her best-friend for Christmas?"

Phew! Finally, a question I didn't know the answer to. A question I *couldn't possibly* know the answer to. What a relief! I was dreading being the headmaster of my own…

Wait. What was going on in my head? My brain was frantically flicking through every page of the last six books, searching for clues so I could answer the question.

Stop, stop, stop!

"On page 12 of book two," I rambled, unable to keep the words from spilling out of my mouth, "Angel asks her best-friend, Precious, what she wants more than anything else in the world, to which Precious replies, "I want to dance on stage with the Bolshoi Ballet." But we all know *that's* never going to happen, because Precious can't even perform a simple pas de bourée on demi-pointe without suffering a syndesmotic ankle sprain – page 94, book one – plus, it's not something you buy as a gift."

The headmaster gazed wistfully up at the ceiling, seemingly lost in a moment.

"No, but it *is* the sort of wonderfully impossible thing Angel would *like* to do for her friend," he said.

"Remember when she arranged for Precious to tap-dance with a princess?"

I did remember. It was hideous.

"Sir," I said, "did you *write* these books or something?"

"Of course not," he answered, a little too quickly. "Just because I have the only copy of an unpublished book, does that mean I'm the author of it?"

"Actually, sir, I think it does."

"Billy, are you suggesting I've sat here for the last thirty years writing books about ballet dancers instead of running this school?"

"Well, it would explain why all the teachers are so useless, sir."

"SCURVY PARROT-FACED RAPSCALLION!" shouted Mr Sampson.

"They are?" frowned the headmaster. "Oh. Well, be that as it may, we must focus on the task in hand, Billy. Now, what did Angel buy her best-friend for her birthday?"

The pages turned in my head.

"Well, in book five the storyline is largely focused on Precious losing her pencil case," I said. "Although quite how anyone can write an entire book about a lost pencil case, I really don't know. I mean, there are three whole chapters about how she left her lip-gloss in there."

"Your point being...?" asked Mr Merriford, a little defensively.

"My point being that Precious has never replaced either of them. So, I think that's the answer. Angel Twinkletoes bought her best-friend a new pencil case and a lip-gloss for her birthday."

The headmaster's face turned grey.

"Ah, but what *kind* of lip-gloss?"

"Cocoa butter, the same as the one she lost. And the pencil-case will be pink, obviously, and it'll probably have the Bolshoi Ballet logo on it."

I thought the headmaster would cry, but instead he muttered, "One question left. Only one question left," and fanned himself with his puzzle book.

The sound of rustling came from the corner of the office. Mr Sampson was distracting himself from the whole awful situation by digging for buried treasure in a small waste paper basket.

"Billy," said Mr Merriford, "would you mind waiting outside for a few minutes whilst I make a quick phone call? I need some help with my final question."

"Of course, sir. *Or* I could go back to class and forget the whole thing?"

"No, Billy, a deal's a deal and I am nothing but a

man of my word. Please wait outside and I'll call you back in when I'm ready."

As I stood in the corridor that day, my brain raced through a hundred thoughts at a million miles an hour. Should I tell Mr Merriford what I'd found in the mud? Should I show him the recipe and admit what I'd done? It was right there, in the back pocket of my trousers (I'd put it there for safe-keeping, along with a bit of spaghetti hoop sandwich I was saving for later), so I could go into the office, hand him the recipe and end this whole thing in the blink of an eye. Then the headmaster could go back to his crossword puzzles and I could go back to…

I could go back to *what?* Being picked on and tormented every day of my life? I couldn't do it. I just couldn't. I felt sorry for Mr Merriford, really I did, but this recipe was my only chance to beat the school bullies. With my boosted brain I could wipe that lip-glossy smirk from Dana Aintree's face and turn Robert's insides to jelly. I could staple Mrs Granger to a wall and shout, "MY NAME IS BILLY RADCLIFFE, YOU HORRIBLE OLD BULLY, MY NAME IS *BILLY RADCLIFFE!*" You see, it had always been my hopeless dream to stop being bullied, and now, with a little help from Auntie Brenda's Brain Booster Juice, it all felt a tiny bit possible.

"You can come in again, Billy," called the headmaster, once my five minutes of corridor-freedom were up. "I've spoken to a friend of mine who works in America for an agency called NASA."

"The National Aeronautics and Space Administration of the United States Federal Government, sir?"

"Yes, yes, I thought you may have heard of it. Anyway, she's given me a question that no ten-year-old boy can possibly know the answer to – not even *you,* Billy Radcliffe. I have it written down on this piece of paper," and he held up a crumpled page from his notepad. "But of course, if by any slim chance you *do* know the answer, I will happily step down from my position as headmaster and admit that the better man won."

"Okay, sir," I said, cringing at what was about to come out of my mouth, "but technically, in our current society, I'm not legally a man until the age of eighteen. Sorry, sir."

Mr Merriford pulled himself up in his chair, nodding seriously.

"Quite right," he agreed, "quite right. Okay, here we go," and he took a long, steadying breath. "Billy, what is the average atmospheric sea-level pressure on the planet Mars?"

I felt the answer swell in the back of my throat.

Think about ordinary things, I told myself. *Think about Curly and the Birdasaurus Pex and playing in mud and dirt, then perhaps the answer will shrink back down to wherever it—*

"NINE MILLIBARS!" The words shot out of me like a jacket potato from a spud-cannon. "That's 0.13 pounds per square inch, sir," I added, miserably.

There was a moment of silence. Then the headmaster closed his puzzle book like it was the last thing he would ever do and rose soberly out of his chair.

"Billy Radcliffe," he said, "in three long decades of teaching, I have never met a child such as you."

"But, sir," I protested, "I don't *want* to be a headmaster! I don't even *like* crossword puzzles!"

"No-one *wants* to be a headmaster, Billy. It just, sort of, happens. Your classmates are going to be thrilled."

"My classmates are going to destroy me," I muttered.

"And if things go wrong, remember these words of wisdom: if at first you don't succeed—"

"I know, try, try again."

Mr Merriford wrinkled his forehead.

"No," he said, with a look of confusion. "If at first you don't succeed, tell everyone you're busy and hide under your desk. It's always worked for me," and then, with one last pat of my head, he left the office muttering, "Nine millibars. Who'd have guessed it? Billy Radcliffe, that's who. The boy's a genius, an absolute genius."

6

A STICKY SITUATION

When the bell sounded for lunchtime play, I ran outside to my corner of the playground. I needed to tell someone what had happened and there was only one person I could trust.

"Curly," I panted, "Curly, where are you? You'll never guess what's happened – it's the worst thing *ever.*"

Robert Williams jabbed me between the shoulder blades, as Dana Aintree watched on with happiness.

"Oi, worm boy, en't our class good enuff for ya no more? Whadda ya reckon, Dana, should I thump 'im or wha'?"

"You can't," I blurted, my boosted brain still talking with a mind of its own. "If you hit me, you'll be put in detention."

"What *are* you *on* about?" whined Dana. "Robert *always* thumps you and he's *never* been put in detention *before.*"

"No, because Mr Merriford was too busy writing books about ballet dancers to notice. But from now on, anyone caught bullying will be put in detention because…because…" No, Billy, don't say it, don't say it! "…because I'm your new headmaster."

CRINGE.

Dana Aintree rolled her eyes so far back in her head she would've seen her own brain if she'd had one.

"Oh *Billy*, you've sunk to a *new* level of *thickness*, really you have. There's Joseph *Compton,* Colin *Bradley*, clever *monkeys, dung* beetles with a *calculator*, and then *you,* Billy *Sad*cliffe." Oh good, the nickname had caught on. And then, "Listen to *this,* everyone," she squealed like a helium-filled pig. "Billy *Sad*cliffe thinks he's the new head *teacher*. What an *idiot!*"

A hoard of children surrounded my corner, all jeering and pointing and chanting, "Sad-*cliffe!* Sad-*cliffe!* Sad-*cliffe!*" when suddenly Mr Sampson came charging out of the school building, hurling potatoes at the sea of heads as if they were coconuts in a shy.

BOOF! BOOF! BOOF! BOOF! BOOF!

"Everyone calm down!" he shouted, ignoring his own instruction. "Or I'll give all of you – THE BLACK SPOT, YARGH! – a silent detention for the rest of break."

"That's it, sir," laughed Robert, "stick the lyin' toe-rag in detention. Whack 'im wiv yer ruler. Teach 'im a lesson. I'll do it if ya want, sir."

The teacher turned his back on the group.

"*That* one deserves a double detention," he said, staring me straight in the eye. "Detention for everyone, sir, and double for him. Don't you agree, Headmaster?"

"Oh my *days,*" smirked Dana, "did you *hear* what he just called *Billy?* Mr Sampson has *finally* lost his last *marble,* the silly old *fool.*"

"Are you listening to this, sir? She called me a silly old fool. I know you're in charge, sir, but I strongly advise that you make the whole school – WALK THE PLANK! – spend their lunchtime sitting quietly in the assembly hall. What do you say, Headmaster?"

When the teacher called me Headmaster for a second time, the laughter faded to a few nervous giggles. Then there were whisperings and mutterings and lowered eyebrows, all of which were nicely rounded off by the sound of Dana trying to piece together a full sentence.

"Is he *actually*— I mean, he can't *really* be— He's not the— This is a *joke,* right?" she managed.

"I assure you it's not," replied Mr Sampson. "The

headmaster wants everyone in the assembly hall for the rest of breaktime, as a punishment for – PINCHIN' ME GOLD DOUBLOONS! – calling me names. Isn't that right, Headmaster, sir?"

"I suppose so," I said. "If you think that's best, Mr Sampson."

The playground groaned and a hundred eyes glared in my direction.

"Well, you heard the headmaster," said the teacher. "Off you go."

"Yes, erm, off you go," I echoed, uncertainly.

"And sit quietly once you get there," he added.

"Yes, sit quietly."

"And the headmaster will be along shortly to supervise you."

"The headmaster will be along shortly to— *What?!*"

The teacher's eyebrows dropped to a deep furrow.

"*You* gave the detention, sir, *you* supervise it."

"But it was your idea!"

"Staff rules, sir, staff rules. You can't expect us teachers to – FLOG THE LITTLE BLIGHTERS WITH A CAT O' NINE TAILS! – bear the brunt of your harsh disciplinary actions, Headmaster. Not on our wages," and as the school filed grumbling into the hall, Mr Sampson headed back to the staffroom.

Well, this wasn't *quite* how I'd thought my Brain Booster adventure would unfold. It was one thing standing up to the bullies, but it was another thing standing up to the whole school at once. At the very least, I was in for a thumping from Robert Williams.

But to my surprise, as I crept nervously into the hall, I found the other children sitting quietly in rows, no-one uttering a word. I walked onto the stage and sat in the headmaster's grand wooden chair. Not a peep. I leant back and put my feet up on Mrs Granger's piano stool. Nothing. And so, for the following hour, I sat like a king on my royal throne as the minutes ticked silently by, until my confidence had grown to the size of a small elephant.

"Okay, everyone, back to class," I instructed, at the sound of the end-of-lunch bell. "I think we've all learnt a very valuable lesson today. Now, if you'll excuse me, I have a very important crossword puzzle to—"

Colin Bradley leapt to his feet.

"DON'T GET UP, BILLY! STAY WHERE YOU ARE!"

"Colin? What's wrong?"

"Oh, nothing," he said, trying to be casual and failing. "You just have to stay where you are because…because…I need you to tell me about square roots! Yes, that's it, square roots."

"You do *not,*" snapped Dana Aintree. "You're just *messing* about. Stop *wasting* the headmaster's *time,* Colin, and sit *down.*"

"It's all right, Dana," I told her, "I'm happy to help. After all, I *am* the headmaster," and I pulled myself proudly up in my wooden chair. "So, to find a square root, you divide the number by its—" Colin Bradley was shaking his rear end like a giant maraca. It was a bit distracting. "I mean, a square root is when a number is multiplied by the— When you multiply the number by its—" Now he was prodding it with an outstretched finger and wagging it like a tail. "A square root is when you— You find a square root by—" Actually, it wasn't even his finger doing the prodding. It was a glue-stick. "A square root is— To find a square root you can— Square roots are when you— Colin, what on *earth* are you doing?"

"I'm not doing anything," he replied, wriggling around as if he had fleas in his underpants. "I'm just trying to concentrate on what you're saying. You know, so it STICKS in my head."

"Shut *up*, Colin," snarled Dana.

"Yeah, shut it, Stinko," added Robert, "or I'll 'ave to thump ya."

But there was no stopping him.

"Let's not get STUCK on the subject of what I'm doing, Headmaster," said Colin. "In fact, if I were you, I would slowly UN-STICK myself out of the SEATuation altogether."

"What? Colin, look, let me come over so I can explain it better and—"

"NO, STAY IN YOUR CHAIR! I mean, why are you so STUCK on the idea of standing up, sir? It's like you're GLUED to the subject of standing. Why not just STICK to sitting down instead, eh?"

"Colin, this is ridiculous. I'm coming over to talk to you and that's—"

"NOOOOOOOOOOO!"

And then I heard it. The worse, most sickening noise I had ever heard. The sound of my trousers tearing in two.

RI-I-I-I-I-I-I-I-I-I-IPPPPP!

A tsunami of laughter filled the hall, smacking me in the face with its spiteful, uncaring hands, flooding my ears like thunder. I looked down. The seat of my trousers was stuck to the wooden chair and my bright orange pants were the only thing keeping me decent. They had glow-in-the-dark stars on them. Mum bought them in a charity shop.

Colin Bradley sped to my side, scuttling across

the hall and up onto the stage, where he stared at my pants in horror.

"I tried to warn you, Billy," he gasped. "Was it not very clear?"

"Not very clear? Colin, why didn't you just *tell me* they'd put glue on my chair?"

"Robert Williams said he'd thump me if I told. He'll thump me anyway now, won't he?"

"Probably," I sighed. "But don't worry, I'll make sure you're okay. Listen, please can you walk behind me while I get back to the office? If you walk close enough, it'll hide my pants." I lowered my voice to a whisper. "They've got glow-in-the-dark stars on them."

"Course, Billy. I used to have a pair just like those. Dad gave mine to a charity shop though."

Marvellous.

Our awkward journey out of the hall, over the playground and along the corridor to the headmaster's office felt like a very long, very strange trek across the Andes. But when we finally got there, I gave Colin an 'I Helped Today' sticker as a thank you and then sent him off to his classroom with a promise that Robert Williams would go back in detention if he so much as threatened to thump him.

Quickly, I pulled the lost property box out from

one of the cupboards. There was only one pair of trousers in it and the label said 'age 4 to 5 years', but at least my fluorescent pants weren't visible from space anymore. I was starting to *hate* being a headmaster. There was only one thing for it – I would write my letter of resignation and quit.

Dear School, I wrote, I do not want to be the Headmarster anymore because the other children have stuck me to a chair.

I scribbled out the word Headmarster. It didn't look right. Headmastor. That didn't look right either. Headmarstor. That was even worse!

And then…

CHING!

The penny dropped.

I couldn't spell headmaster. Why couldn't I spell headmaster? Yesterday I could spell rhododoodydah (or something like that) and now I couldn't spell my own job. Plus, now I came to think of it, why hadn't I been able to tell Colin Bradley what a square root was? Square roots are obviously something to do with square plants, but for the life of me I couldn't think what.

"Oh no," I breathed, "the Brain Booster has worn off – I'm the world's most stupid headmaster. I need to send a teacher out for more ingredients before anyone finds out about the Juice. Now, where's my recipe?"

Hurriedly, I reached into the back pocket of my trousers. What were all these football stickers doing in here? I mean, seriously, what sort of a person goes around putting football stickers in someone else's—

ARRRRRRRRRGH!

"These are someone else's trousers!" I cried. "These are someone else's pockets! Mine are still stuck to the headmaster's chair!" and with no thought for how silly I looked like in my teeny-tiny uniform, I ran from the office, down the corridor, across the playground and into the school hall, where I found the back of my trousers still glued to the seat of the chair.

"Dana and Robert have messed with the wrong trousers this time," I muttered, tugging at the material until I could just about squeeze my hand into the pocket.

There was a used tissue, a shrivelled-up conker, a stale sandwich crust and a crumpled Birdasaurus Pex – *where was the recipe?* I double-checked, throwing the contents all over the floor in my panic, until my pockets were as empty as my brain.

But the recipe and all the marvellous-ness that went with it had gone.

7

THE SCHOOL INSPECTOR

Ten minutes later I had taken Mr Merriford's advice and was hiding under my office desk, when somebody knocked on the door.

KNOCK! KNOCK!

"I'm busy!" I called, trying to sound casual. "Come back when I've finished my puzzle please!" The handle turned and the door clicked open. "Hey, I told you I'm busy – go back to class or I'll get Mr Sampson to throw a potato at you."

The upside-down head of a small, beetle-like woman appeared from above the desk. A huge pair of glasses swung from her face, magnifying her eyes to the size of tennis balls. It was like being watched by a trout.

"It's no use hiding," she said. "I've seen it all before. Last week, I found the headmistress of St Jiminy's in a wheelie bin. I'm here to inspect the school, Headmaster, and inspect the school is what I shall do."

Just when I thought today couldn't get any

worse.

Quickly, I scrambled out from the desk, smacking my head on the swivel chair and sending it crashing into the bookcase. An avalanche of books tumbled down on my head.

THUD! THUD! THUD! THUD! THUD!

The Inspector made a note of it on her clipboard.

"I'm going to ask you a series of questions," she told me. I hoped they were easier than Mr Merriford's because my brain wasn't up to answering anything much at the moment. "Firstly, why are your trousers too small for your legs?"

"Because it makes me feel like a giant," I joked, trying to lighten the mood.

The Inspector pulled a face as if I had sworn at her.

"Why do you look like you're ten years old?"

"Because…I'm ten years old."

"How long have you been the head teacher of this school?"

I added it up on my fingers.

"Half a day."

"Did you get this job through the usual processes?"

"Yes. I won it in a quiz."

"What are your qualifications?"

"What are my *whats?*"

"What do you have in the way of certificates?"

"Well, I came fifth in the egg and spoon race three years ago. You had to be fourth to get a certificate, but Mrs Granger gave me a sticker. It said 'Loser' on it, but still…"

"Do you have a BEd, a PGCE, or a PhD?"

"No, but a man on the phone said my mum might have PPI."

"And finally, am I being secretly filmed for a spoof television programme in which a ten-year-old boy pretends to be the headmaster of his own school for a bit of a laugh?"

I scanned the office for cameras.

"I hope not," I whispered, "I was picking my nose under that table."

The Inspector curled her rubbery lips up over her nostrils, where they sat on her thick glasses like a slug on a greenhouse window.

"You can show me around the classrooms now," she said, and she scuttled down the corridor like a cockroach.

The first classroom we came to was Mrs Granger's. We arrived to find her leaning over Joseph Compton with her stapler in hand, but spotting the Inspector she immediately became the nicest, happiest, most joyful teacher you could ever wish to imagine.

It was like watching a velociraptor dance the polka.

"I've been teaching my lovely class all about Romans," she sang, skipping towards a display of mosaics and showing them off as if they were a prize on a TV gameshow. "Children, who can tell the Inspector what we've learnt about Ancient Rome?"

"Rome is in *Italy*," offered Dana Aintree. "It used to be an *empire*."

"Excellent!" cheered Mrs Granger. "You're a clever, *clever* girl, Dana What's-Your-Pretty-Little-Face. Anyone else?"

Robert Williams stood up and cleared his throat. He was either about to make a speech or spit at someone.

"Augustus woz the first leader of the Roman Empire. He came into power in 27BC and he 'ad a special group of soldiers oo protected 'im called the Praetorian Guard."

The Inspector scribbled something down on her clipboard.

"Very good, Robert!" said Mrs Granger. "Take a house-point!"

But the boy hadn't finished.

"Augustus woz born on 23rd September 63BC," he went on. "He woz the great-nephew of Julius Caesar. In 31BC, he defeated Antony and Cleopatra at the Battle of Actium, which is 'ow he become the undisputed leader of Rome."

"Splendid!" cried Mrs Granger. "Ten house points! No, twenty! No, thirty! Anyone else know some facts about—"

"There woz another famous Roman called Quintus Horatius Flaccus, oo joined the Roman Army under General Brutus. He woz also a very talented poet and a member of a literary circle what included such great names as Virgil and Macenas. He wrote four books of odes, a book of epodes and two books of satires. Other examples of satire are *Gulliver's Travels* by Jonathan Swift, *Nineteen Eighty-Four* by George Orwell, Thomas Nast's political cartoons against Boss Tweed and—"

CHING!

That was the sound of the penny dropping for the second time in one day.

"He's stolen my recipe!" I bellowed across the room.

The Inspector's eyes swelled behind her glasses. She looked like a goldfish in a bowl.

"Headmaster, do you teach cookery as well as

running the school?" she asked.

"No, it's just, I recently lost a recipe and I think this boy might've taken it."

"What sort of a recipe?"

"A recipe for crab-eye soup," I told her, still trying to keep my Brain Booster Juice a secret. "It's Japanese."

The Inspector blinked and her own eye-balls wobbled like two bowls of jelly.

She turned to Mrs Granger.

"Teacher," she said, "is your current headmaster a little bit…you know?"

"Thick?" Mrs Granger asked, spitefully. "Yes."

"Then I suggest we temporarily replace him with somebody clever so your school doesn't fail its inspection. Your thoughts, please."

"I think that's a wonderful idea," agreed Mrs Granger. "Do you have someone brainy in mind?"

My stomach turned. No, no, no, this can't be happening, *this can't be happening!*

"Well," began the Inspector, "if it's cleverness we're looking for, it seems to me there is only choice."

"Oh, I appreciate the offer," blushed Mrs Granger, "but I'm far too busy teaching to be the new—"

"Not you." The Inspector turned to Robert

Williams. No, please, I'm begging you, anyone but him, *anyone!* "You there, unusually large boy, how would you like to be the new temporary headmaster of this school?"

NOOOOOOOOOOO!

Robert Williams grinned widely.

"Wicked," he said. "Cheers very much," and the other children swarmed over to congratulate him. The hideous boy pumped both fists in the air like he'd just won the World Cup. "Looks like *I'm* the clever one now, eh, Sadcliffe?" he smirked, as Mrs Granger showed the Inspector out of the room. "And as I'm in charge, I reckon it's time we 'ad a bit more fun at this school, don't you?"

8

A STRANGER AT THE GATE

Dana Aintree was in the playground when I arrived at school the next day. A swarm of children were buzzing around her like wasps on a donut, as she preened herself like an ornamental duck.

"Robert Williams is *perfect* for the job," she quacked, brushing her hair with a pink mermaid comb. "I've *always* thought he would make a *brilliant* head teacher. Is my *lipstick* on right?"

It wasn't. But twelve people nodded anyway.

The bell sounded and we all lined-up, ready to face our first day with Robert Williams as the new headmaster, when suddenly the boy's bulging face sprung out of an upstairs window like a fat gargoyle.

"Whadda ya think yer doin'?" he bawled "Anyone caught linin' up will be locked in the store cupboard and made to eat slugs," and at once the playground burst into chaos as two hundred children ran into school, all shouting and hollering and squawking like crows.

When the teachers heard the commotion, an echo of demands rang down the corridor…

"NO RUNNING INSIDE!"

"STOP MAKING THAT NOISE!"

"DON'T SWING ON THE DOORS!"

"GET DOWN FROM THOSE SHELVES!"

"DO *NOT* THROW THAT CHAIR!"

"WOULD YOU *PUT* THAT LIBRARIAN *DOWN?!"*

Of course, Mrs Granger was by far the angriest. She was smouldering at her desk when we entered the classroom, burning with rage, as if she would self-combust at any given moment.

Not that anyone cared. Dana Aintree had swiped a crate full of milk-cartons from the back of the school and was now launching them one by one across the room like water-bombs.

SPLURGE! SPLURGE! SPLURGE! SPLURGE!

No-one was a big fan of school milk, especially the slightly curdled sort we were made to drink during the summer, so the rest of us joined in too.

SPLURGE! SPLURGE! SPLURGE! SPLURGE!

Then a group from Mr Sampson's class heard the racket and the girl called Sally rushed in with her own crate of ammunition.

SPLURGE! SPLURGE! SPLURGE! SPLURGE!

After which the Reception children, being young and impressionable, also appeared.

SPLURGE! SPLURGE! SPLURGE! SPLURGE!

And soon it became the biggest milk-bomb fight the world had ever seen.

SPLURGE! SPLURGE! SPLURGE! SPLURGE!

Our teacher leapt to her feet in a fiery explosion of fury.

"STOP THAT, YOU HORRIBLE LITTLE BRATS, OR I'LL STAPLE YOU UP BY THE—"

SPLURGE!

The carton struck on the side of Mrs Granger's head. It burst open like a coconut and the contents streamed down the creases of her neck in rivers, her soggy chin-skin trembling like a lit firework.

"Oh *look,*" mocked Dana, "the *milk* has gone back to the *cow.*"

GASP!

Everyone froze. No-one had ever dared speak to Mrs Granger like that before.

"Are you talking to *me?*" seethed the teacher.

"Do you *see* anyone *else* being an annoying old *bat?*"

DOUBLE GASP!

Mrs Granger growled in the back of her throat.

"How would you like to spend your entire weekend hanging from a display board, Dana What's-Your-Face?"

"And how would *you* like to spend *your* weekend ironing out your wrinkly old *neck?*" came the reply.

TRIPLE GASP!

Every drop of blood the teacher's body shot to her face, where it boiled violently under her skin like an enormous stewing tomato.

"Headmaster's office," she rumbled, her knuckles turning white as they gripped the desk. "Now!"

"Ho *hum,*" sang Dana, "as you *wish,*" and she skipped out of the classroom without a care in the world.

Mrs Granger leant back in her chair, gasping for air and gulping down great mouthfuls of black-coffee, before hurling the empty mug at Joseph Compton. It skimmed the top of his head and smashed through a window behind him.

"Flippin' heck," muttered Joseph, "what did *I* do?"

Suddenly, the great bulk of Robert Williams appeared in the doorway like a total eclipse of the classroom. He was scoffing a family-size bar of chocolate with Dana Aintree at his side, as happy as a monkey at banana-camp.

"Oi, Mrs Gee, I needs a word wiv ya." The boy wiped his chocolatey mouth on the sleeve of his jumper and Mrs Granger's face twitched. I could see she wanted to throw something at him. "Dana reckons ya've stopped 'er milk-fight. Is that right?"

"Ye-e-e-e-e-e-e-e-s," said the teacher through gritted teeth, sounding very much like a creaky door.

"Well, ya'd better say sorry or I'll 'ave to sack ya."

Mrs Granger's face dropped. She hugged her precious stapler like a baby, and then, with a look that said she would rather be pulling out her own teeth, she muttered something under her breath.

It could've been, "Sorry." Then again, it could've been, "Sausage."

"We can't 'ear ya, Mrs Gee," said Robert. "Ya'll 'ave to speak up."

Calmly, Mrs Granger put down her stapler. She walked towards Dana Aintree, cupped both hands to her mouth and went, *"SO-RRRRRRYYYYYY!"* right in the girl's face. "There," she huffed. "Said it. Now, if you'll excuse me, I have some Romans to teach about."

"No, ya don't," replied Robert. "We en't learnin'

about Romans no more, we're learnin' about the Middle Ages. And this afternoon, we're 'aving a joustin' tournament."

"Jousting?" gaped Mrs Granger. "Have you done a risk assessment for that?"

"Yeah, and it's gunna be really risky so it should be loads o' fun. I en't got no suits of armour though, Mrs Gee, so I needs ya to make one, all right?"

"Don't be absurd," she scoffed. "How on earth am I meant to do that? I don't have an endless supply of craft resources just lying around my classroom, you know."

An idea spread like fungus on Dana Aintree's face.

"Yes, you *do,*" she smirked. "You can *use* all these stinky *milk-cartons*."

"A suit of armour made out of milk cartons? Dana What's-Your-Face, that's an absolutely—"

"Wicked idea," grinned Robert. "Don't wash 'em though, Mrs Gee. The stinkier, the better," and I didn't like the way his eyes turned to *me* when he said that.

Colin Bradley sat dismally on my wall that lunchtime. He was holding a wet paper-towel on his thumb and eating a tub of cockles.

"Wotcha, Billy. Rubbish day, isn't it?"

"The worst," I said. "What's wrong with your thumb?"

"Robert's had me cutting up gym mats all morning with a pair of plastic scissors."

He peeled away the paper towel to reveal a scissor-shaped indent in his hand.

"Ouch," I said. "Why does he want the gym mats cut up? If he doesn't want them, why doesn't he just chuck them in the wheelie bins with the library books?"

"That's what *I* said. I said, 'Mr Williams, sir, how about I just roll them up and chuck them in the wheelie-bins with the library books, sir?' That's when he took the big metal scissors away and made me use the plastic ones instead." The boy sighed heavily. "And I reckon you were right about him stealing your soup recipe, Billy. After he stuck you to that chair yesterday, he made me go home to fetch him some pickled eels and crab-eyes."

At that moment, Robert Williams climbed onto my wall wearing a long, red robe and a gold paper crown.

"Pipe down, you lot!" he yelled. The playground silenced and a sea of excited faces gazed up at him. "The joustin' tournament's about to start. I'm gunna be the king, obviously, and I've chosen four people to do the joustin'. The first two are Dana Aintree and Sally Jones."

Dana's friends formed a circle and began an endless Mexican wave, while the girl called Sally's friends performed a very bad cheerleader dance using hair scrunchies as pom-poms.

"Billy," whispered Colin, "what's a jousting tournament?"

"I think it's when two people knock each other off horses with a big stick," I said.

"Oh," replied Colin. "Where's he going to get two horses from?"

"And the other contestants," announced Robert, "are Billy Radcliffe and Colin Bradley."

Colin leapt from the wall and seized me like a giant fishfinger sandwich.

"We've been picked, we've been picked! I've never been picked for *anything* before! Isn't it wonderful, Billy, isn't it great?!"

"Erm, Colin, I don't think Robert would choose us for anything *good*."

Colin nodded.

"You're right," he agreed. And then, "If he's picked Dana Aintree it'll be *better than good!*" and he danced towards the assembly hall as if all his dreams were about to come true.

As the playground emptied, Curly's head popped up from the soil.

"Oh, Curly," I said, "I wish I was small like you. Then I could hide in one of your worm holes so no-one could find me. Or, even better, if you were big like me, we could say you were a bully-munching Birdasaurus Pex and no-one would pick on me ever again."

A hungry blackbird flitted onto the grass. It tilted its head from side to side, picturing my best-friend in an extra-long hot-dog bun, so I shooed it away and was covering Curly with a leaf when a movement caught my eye from the metal gates of the school playground.

Outside on the pavement, an old woman was staring in through the bars. She was very small with a mess of silver-blue curls on the top of her head and a face like a porcelain doll. She didn't smile, she didn't move, she didn't speak. She just stood there unblinkingly, like a mannequin in a shop window, until suddenly from the pocket of her oversized coat she produced a single sheet of paper.

The old woman lifted the page into the air. A breeze caught hold of it, carrying it through the bars of the gate and lifting it over the playground like an autumn leaf. So graceful was its dance, so mesmerising – two circles to the left, two circles to the right, two circles to the left, two circles to the right – that I didn't notice how close it was getting until it was flat on my face.

Startled, I snatched down the page and stared at the writing.

"I don't believe it," I breathed. "I actually don't believe it. It's another copy of the recipe. Auntie Brenda has brought it to me herself. I have to thank her, I have to ask her how she—"

But when I looked back to the gate, the street was empty and the old woman had gone.

9

COLIN THE SMELLY

"Yer late!" bawled Robert, as I charged through the double doors of the school hall. The recipe was folded up in my fist and it would stay there until I was safely at home. I couldn't risk losing it twice in one week. "Fetch yer costume, Sadcliffe, and 'urry up. I wants ya to be one of the 'orses."

What a surprise.

Not.

My horse costume was furry and brown, with an orange stain down the front. Someone had stapled a couple of toilet-roll tubes to a headband for ears. I looked more like a hairy robot than a horse.

The hall cheered when I put it on. Even Mrs Granger joined in.

"Ra, ra, ra," she droned, from the back of the hall. "Whoop, whoop. Hurray. Yippee."

She was sitting with the other teachers, cross-legged on the floor in a long row, staring up at the hall clock.

TICK, TICK, TICK, TICK…

That was strange.

"Let the joustin' begin!" cried Robert, straightening his crown. "Our first contestant, is *DANA THE DREADFUL!*"

This was Dana's cue to come out from behind the piano in her canteen dinner-tray suit of armour. The metal trays had been welded to fit the horrible girl like a glove and the cup holders had been cut out to make eyeholes in her face-shield – it didn't take a genius to figure out who had been clever enough to do *that*. In one hand, she was holding her lance (a mop handle), in the other she clung to her shield (a dustbin lid), and she strutted across the hall like a catwalk model.

"Do you *have* to call me *dreadful?*" she whined, as she reached Robert Williams's chair. "It's not very *nice* to call people *names,* Robert."

"It's yer warrior name," explained the boy. "There were a famous Muscovite called Ivan the Terrible coz of 'is victory at Kazan in 1552 and he were really scary, so I thought you should 'ave a name too."

"Oh," beamed the girl. She didn't know what he was talking about, but she liked the sound of it. "In *that* case – let's *hear* it for Dana the *Dreadful!*"

"Ra, ra, ra. Whoop whoop. Hurray. Yippee," went the teachers.

"Now, *where's* my trusty *steed?*" she grinned, and she smirked in my direction.

GULP!

At that moment the girl called Sally trotted out on all fours wearing the front half of an old pantomime horse costume. Dana leapfrogged onto her back and Sally whinnied happily. I was so grateful neither one of them was my partner, even though there was bound to be some horrible reason why Robert had paired me with…

"COLIN THE SMELLY!" cried the boy.

"Ra, ra, ra," droned the teachers. "Whoop, whoop. Hurray. Yippee."

As Colin stepped out from behind the piano, his face flushed pink. He was wearing a milk-carton suit of armour. It was so bulky he couldn't bend his arms or his legs. Plus, to make matters worse, he left a trail of milk as he waddled along.

"You look…big," I said, trying not to grimace.

"I look like a wally," he replied, as the school guffawed at his costume. "Why are you wearing a piece of Mrs Granger's carpet?"

I'd thought that orange stain looked familiar.

"I'm a horse," I said, glumly. "In fact, I'm *your*

horse. Sit on my back like Dana's doing with Sally."

"Oh, I dunno, Billy, I'm rubbish at riding horses. A dolphin, on the other hand, now a dolphin I *can* ride."

"I'm afraid you don't have a choice, Colin. And it's not like I'm an *actual* horse, is it? All you have to do is sit on my back, hold out your lance and— Wait, is that your lance?" He was holding a strip of gym mat. The end was bent over like a limp banana. "That's *it?* That's all they've given you? You don't even have a shield."

"ON YER MARKS…" began Robert.

"It's starting! Quick, Colin, get on my back!"

"GET SET…"

"Colin, hurry! *Hurry!*"

"CHA-A-A-A-A-A-ARGE!"

The girl called Sally galloped towards us with Dana Aintree perched on her back like something out of a spaghetti western film. Colin screamed. Then he jumped in the air and landed with one leg over each of my shoulders. The milk-cartons under his buttocks burst like a couple of sour milk stink-bombs and the smell of it made me gag, watering my eyes, and when my vision cleared Dana's lance was already there in my face so…I ducked. I ducked and the mop-handle skimmed past my head, struck Colin on the arm and the boy came crashing down to the floor with a yelp.

"Are you alright?" I asked him, as Dana and Sally did a celebratory lap of the hall. "Are you hurt?"

The boy lifted his head and groaned.

SPLAT!

What was that?

SPLAT!

Something soft was hitting me on the back.

SPLAT!

Where were they coming from?

SPLAT!

That one hit Colin on the head.

SPLAT!

It hadn't come from Mr Sampson's spud-cannon.

SPLAT!

He was at the back of the room with the other teachers.

SPLAT!

And then, silence, as if we had just entered the eye of the storm, before Robert cried, *"NOW!"* and the hall erupted into a frenzy of noise.

SPLAT! SPLAT! SPLAT! SPLAT! SPLAT! SPLAT! SPLAT! SPLAT!

Through the roar of voices, the soggy objects flew in from every direction, pelting us, hammering us, blinding us, soaking us, until we were both covered in a sticky mess of red.

"I'm bleeding!" wailed Colin. "I'm bleeding!"

"You're not bleeding," I shouted, as the shower of projectiles kept coming. "They're throwing tomatoes at us. Quick, Colin – behind the piano!"

Scrambling through the slippery gunk to our shelter, we slid to a messy halt on the wooden floor, gasping for breath as the ambush dissolved into laughter. Our names echoed around the hall – "Did you see Billy's face?" "Colin's covered in it!" "I got Sadcliffe five times!" – until Robert gave Dana a trophy and the whole school left as if nothing had happened, as if we weren't still lying there behind the piano, cold and damp and humiliated in our ridiculous costumes.

When the door closed behind them, we were alone.

A heavy tear dripped down Colin's cheek and landed on the back of my hand. As it mixed with the mess of tomatoes, I remembered the recipe still clenched in my fist and a surge of angry determination rushed through my veins.

"Don't cry, Colin," I told him, "everything's going to be all right. I have a plan, a really *good* plan, and I need your help. I need you to get me some more crab-eyes and pickled eels, as many as you can lay your hands on. Can you do that, Colin?"

"I-I suppose," he said, blankly. "I could bring them to school tomorrow."

"Tomorrow's no good, Colin. I need them tonight. Bring them to my house as soon as you can and leave the rest to me. It's time someone put an end to Robert's bullying once and for all."

10

MYSTERY SHOPPER

Mum was engrossed in her poker match with Mrs Pollychamp when I got back from school, so I grabbed my pocket money and ran to The Next-Door Shop for the other Brain Booster ingredients.

"Mustard, garlic, toothpaste," I said, ticking them off on my recipe as I loaded them into my basket. "Now, where are the baked beans?" and soon I had everything I needed.

The counter was near the front of the shop, at the end of the bread aisle. There were all sorts of bread: brown bread, white bread, granary, wholemeal. And there, on the bottom shelf, at the very end of the aisle, a cellophane-wrapped sliced bread with the maker's name printed onto the wrapper.

AUNTIE BRENDA'S
MEDIUM SLICED LOAF

A gazillion goose-bumps popped up on the back of my neck.

POP! POP! POP! POP! POP! POP! POP!

"Can I help you?" came a voice from behind me.

I turned to see a gum-chewing assistant, a tall teenage girl with a single white stripe in her black hair. She looked like the back end of a skunk.

"Where did you get this bread?" I asked.

The shop assistant shoved both hands in her apron pockets and screwed up her nose.

"Well it didn't come from the butcher, did it?"

Wow, this girl was so cool she should've been in the frozen food aisle. And for some reason I thought it would be a good idea to pretend I was cool too, so I tried out some awesome teenagery words I had learnt from the telly.

"Dat wuz well savage," I told her. "I iz owned, fam, in it?"

The shop girl smiled (well, I say 'smile' – it was more of a laugh really).

"I know you. You're Andy Radcliffe's little brother."

"Fer real."

"Sorry?"

"Wicked."

"What?"

"D'you get me?"

"Well, no." She inspected me like a hair she'd just found in her sandwich, and then, "Listen," she said, "I'll let you use my staff discount if you ask your brother to go out with my friend. What do you reckon?"

What did I reckon? I reckoned my ears would shrivel up and drop from the sides of my head, *that's* what I reckoned. Somebody wanted a date with my brother? What *was* the world coming to?

On the other hand, a discount was a discount. And it would mean I'd have enough money left over for a tin of spaghetti hoops, otherwise it would be baked bean sandwiches for the rest of the week and that's just weird.

"All right then," I told her. "I mean, I wouldn't normally inflict my brother on anyone, not unless they deserved it, but I've got triple amounts of ingredients to buy so a discount would be great, thanks."

The shop girl peered into my basket.

"Are those all ingredients? What're you making?"

"Oh, erm, soup."

"With *toothpaste* in it?"

"With…mint in it."

"We do *sell* mint, you know. Like, *actual* mint, as opposed to dental care products."

"Yes, but I use toothpaste for the…cavity protection."

I showed her my mum's best poker face and it must've worked, because after that she didn't ask any more questions about my ingredients. Instead, she beeped them through the till as if she was born to beep food through a till, with one hand scanning the barcodes and the other one twiddling her nose-stud.

At the same time, she was reading a huge book by a man called Leo Tolstoy. It was resting on top of a see-through cabinet, a long refrigerator full of things like sausages, bacon, pies, cheese and fish. And there, propped up on the glass near the salmon, was a drawing of a brain and a hand-written sign saying:

Fresh Fish – Nature's Own Brain Booster!

POP! POP! POP! POP! POP! POP! POP!

That was *two* gazillion goose-bumps popping up on the back of my neck.

"My friend's called Sarah," said the shop girl. "She wrote a poem for your brother. It goes:

Your eyes are so blue,

Your head is a circle,
I think you are cool
Coz your hair is purple.

"I told her 'circle' doesn't rhyme with 'purple', but she wouldn't listen." She noticed me looking at the selection of sea-food. "Please tell me you don't put fish in your toothpaste soup."

"No. Well, actually, yes, but I'm all sorted for fish. I was just looking at your sign. What does it mean by 'brain booster'?"

"It means the omega 3 oil in fish supports your cognitive thinking," said the shop girl. She must've been using some cool teenagery lingo when she said that, because I didn't understand a word of it. "It won't suddenly make you a genius, if that's what you're asking."

"Of course not!" I said, faking a laugh. "What a ridiculous idea!"

The girl lowered her eyebrows and beeped through the last of my ingredients.

"Is that everything?"

"Think so," I replied. "I'll just check my list to make sure."

Unfolding the recipe, I noticed a tomato-coloured stain at the bottom of the page. It must've happened during the jousting tournament. In the middle of the stain was a small hole, where the tomato juice had seeped through the paper. And next to the hole was a tiny dot of ink, as if something else had been written there, as if the final ingredient of my recipe was…

"AAAAAAAARRRRRRRGH!"

"Problem?" glowered the girl.

"The final ingredient of my recipe is missing! What am I going to do? *What am I going to do?!"*

"Well, you could try chilling out for a start. And then you could go home and look in the recipe book."

"But…but…" But *what?* I couldn't tell her my recipe didn't come from a book, that an old woman had magicked it across the playground to me earlier that day. "But…but I don't want to go all the way home and then have to come all the way back again. It'll take too long."

She scowled.

"Don't you live next door?"

A small queue of people had formed behind me. The man at the back tutted impatiently.

"But…but…"

"Look, why not have a think about what you're missing while I serve these other customers? You might remember it if you try," and she smiled at the person behind me. "Yes, madam, just that, is it?"

The customer paid for her shopping and then left the shop.

"But I'm rubbish at thinking," I told her. The man at the back tutted again. "I'll never remember it."

"Then why don't you brave the long and hazardous journey all the way back to *the house next door?*" And then, "Oh no, that lady's left without her shopping," she said, nodding to a family-size bottle of milk on the counter.

A drizzle of condensation ran down the side of the plastic, glistening in the fluorescent lighting, winking a secret only *I* could hear.

"Your missing ingredient," the milk seemed to whisper, *"is ME!"*

"No way," I breathed. "No actual way." The man behind me slammed his packet of biscuits down on the counter and stormed out of the shop. "That woman," I said, "the one who paid for this milk, what did she look like?"

The shop girl shrugged.

"I don't know, old, small, silvery blue hair. Oh, and her face looked a bit like–"

"A porcelain doll," we finished together.

"That's right," she said. "Do you know her?"

"Do I *know* her?" I scoffed, meaning, 'No, not

really, but I'm fairly sure her name's Auntie Brenda and she's left this bottle of milk here for me.' I gave the girl another dose of my best poker face. "I mean, yes, I know her. She's my auntie. I can take it to her, if you like. The milk, I mean."

Again, the girl shrugged.

"If you want," she said, and she popped the milk in a bag. "What about your missing ingredient?"

"Oh, don't worry," I replied, handing over the money, "I've remembered what it is now and I've already got some. Thanks for the discount though – I'll talk to Andy about your friend," and I left the shop with enough Brain Booster ingredients to make *three times* the amount of Juice I had ever made before.

Triple marvellous!

11

THE SECOND BATCH

Dana Aintree wore make-up to school the next day. In fact, Dana Aintree wore *so* much make-up to school the next day she could've joined the circus.

Of course, this type of thing was banned because Mrs Granger was ugly enough as it was without other people wearing make-up and making her look even worse. But today she hadn't noticed. She was too busy scribbling on the whiteboard, writing out long lists of random words before wiping them off with her sleeve and starting all over again.

She didn't even stop when Mandy Langton balanced a pot-plant on her head. Not even when Peter Giselle stuck a marker pen up her nostril. Not even when Robert Williams crashed through the classroom door wearing a fake army uniform and a row of tin-foil medals, shouting, "ATTEN-*TION!*"

"Good morning, Mr Williams," sang the class.

Quite why it was so thrilling to be ordered around by some whopping great thug, I'll never know.

"Actually, it's *Captain* Williams," corrected the boy. "Now, listen up. The teachers are gunna 'ave a talent contest this afternoon and we'll all be watchin'. Mrs Gee's really excited about it, en't ya, Mrs Gee?"

"Ra, ra, ra," went the teacher, her eyes never leaving the pen. "Whoop, whoop. Hurray. Yippee."

The class giggled.

"Oh, and as of today, there's a new school dinner menu, so if ya don't like chocolate ya'd better bring a packed lunch from now on." Then he stamped his foot and shouted, "PLAYTIME 'TIL LUNCH! DIIIIIIS-*MISSED!*" before heading back to his office.

Everyone charged out of the classroom like a herd of wildebeests. But there was something fishy going on with Mrs Granger and I was going to find out what it was.

"Mrs Granger?" I said, peering over her shoulder as the room emptied. Her eyes were more vacant than a cubical with a blocked toilet. "Mrs Granger, why are you writing on that whiteboard?"

There was a large watch on the wrist of her writing hand.

TICK, TICK, TICK, TICK…

"Write on the whiteboard," she said. "Write on the whiteboard."

My triple-boosted brain went into overdrive.

"Mrs Granger," I gabbled, "I think Robert Williams has put you under chronometrical hypnosis by tapping into the prefrontal region of your cerebral cortex, which is why you're following his every command. But he won't get away with it for much longer – I have a plan," and here's where it started.

The first thing I had to do was sneak across the playground, past the other children and into the school canteen. A low wall ran around the edge of the netball court, so I slunk from the building and quickly got down on all fours. It was a beautiful day for crawling behind a wall. The sky was blue, the ground was dry, and I scampered along like an excited puppy, completely unseen, until a dark raincloud suddenly blocked out the light.

"Wotcha you doin' down there, Sadcliffe?" asked the cloud.

Except it wasn't a cloud. It was Robert Williams's fat head.

The sight of it made my brain spin with ideas.

"Captain Williams, sir!" I boomed, jumping to my feet and saluting so hard I poked myself in the eye. "I'm doing my laps, sir! Fifty times around the playground, sir! On my stomach, sir!"

The boy scowled.

"Did *I* tell ya to do that?"

"No, Captain Williams, sir! I ordered myself to do it, sir! As a punishment, sir! For being so stupid, sir!"

"Oh," said the boy, uncertainly. And then, "In that case yer new nickname's gunna be Private Thicko, cuz yer even more stoopid than you was yesterday. Ya'd better answer to it, Sadcliffe, or I'll 'ave to thump ya."

"Yes, Captain Williams, sir! Private Thicko is an excellent name, sir! It's absolutely no more than I'd deserve, sir!"

"Yeah, well," he said, "get on wiv it then, Private Thicko. Double time."

"Sir, yes, sir!" I cried, banging the heels of my shoes together and practically breaking my ankle, before dropping to my stomach and slithering behind the wall like an overgrown worm.

Robert chortled and then moved onto his next victim, so I scrambled up from the ground and darted into the canteen, where the dinner-ladies were sat at one of the tables with a huge pile of chocolate and a big alarm clock in front of them.

TICK, TICK, TICK, TICK…

The first dinner-lady slit open one of the chocolate wrappers and passed it on to the next…

TICK, TICK, TICK, TICK…

Who removed the wrapper and tossed it to the third…

TICK, TICK, TICK, TICK…

Who snapped the chocolate into pieces before handing it over to the fourth…

TICK, TICK, TICK, TICK…

Who slung the whole lot into a big bowl at the end of the table, shouting, *"Robert's the best! Robert's the best!"* whilst waving her 'I ❤ ROBERT' flag.

"Morning, ladies," I smiled, to no reaction. "Do you mind if I go in the kitchen to borrow some equipment? No? Great. Ta very much."

Well, this was *very* exciting. You see, children weren't allowed in the kitchen. It was full of pots and pans and platters of all shapes and sizes, as well as electrical items like toasters, mixers and grills, each of them spotlessly clean and shiny. In fact, when the sunlight came in through the window, the whole room sparkled like a giant disco ball and the dinner-ladies didn't want anyone messing it up with their grubby little fingers.

But I wasn't here to make a mess of the place.

I was here to *demolish* it.

My first job was to remove every screw from every appliance with a butter knife and extract all the wires with a pair of tongs. Then I lit the gas cooker and used the flames to solder the wires into longer lengths, before curling them up into twenty-three piles of snake-like coils.

"Twelve metres of two core black 1mm round cable," I muttered. "Seven metres of three core white 2mm flat oval cable, fifteen metres of coaxial cable…"

It was important I had enough of each wire and at the end of my count I was only short by two metres of copper cable.

Checking the dinner-ladies were still engrossed in their chocolate bars, I went to an old pay-phone on the wall of the kitchen (there was bound to be some behind there). I walloped it down from its brackets with a small wok, then used a fork to dig a hole in the plasterboard, where I found the glorious red and white cable twisted together like a coppery marshmallow treat.

"Erm, you might not want to watch this next bit," I told the dinner-ladies, swapping my wok for a large rolling pin. "It's for a good cause though, I promise."

Time to hammer out the baking trays!

Now, the dinner-ladies looked after their baking trays better than they looked after us. Each one shone like a mirror, and when they served your lunch from them you were told not to touch them because they were hot. That was a lie. You were told not to touch them because the dinner-ladies didn't *want* you to touch them, and if you dared go near them you'd be struck down by the legendary curse of the Dinner-Lady Clan and the taste of semolina would stay in your mouth forever.

At least, that's what Joseph Compton says anyway.

But Robert Williams was much scarier than any curse, so I snatched up every baking tray I could find and flattened them out with the rolling pin. Then I shoved them all into bin bags and dragged them out of a fire exit at the back of the canteen, where a flight of emergency steps went up the outside wall to an upstairs storage room.

Carefully, one bag at a time, I carried the wires and screws and trays up the steps and onto the corrugated iron roof, where I pieced together the most marvellous contraption ever known to man, a magnificent structure with the power to end Robert's reign of our school forever – and then all I had to do, was wait.

12

DISH OF THE DAY

The talent contest took place amongst the sticky, tomatoey mess of yesterday's jousting tournament. No-one had cleaned it up because the maintenance man had been hypnotised into polishing the toilet floor with his own toothbrush instead. The teachers lined up on the stage like lemmings on a clifftop, their eyebrows twitching in time with the clock on the back wall of the room.

TICK, TICK, TICK, TICK…

"First up," announced Robert, using Dana's pink mermaid comb as a fake microphone, "it's Miss Crawford!"

"Yaaaaay!" cheered the crowd.

"Ra, ra, ra," droned the teachers. "Whoop, whoop. Hurray. Yippee."

"Miss Crawford," grinned the boy, wickedly, "be a frog."

Something changed in the woman's eyes. Her mouth turned down at the edges and she dropped to the floor with her knees turned out, going, "Rrrrribbit, rrrrribbit," then she hopped around the stage, croaking loudly and belching in between, until Robert Williams pulled a jam jar out from under his chair.

He took off the lid and a large bluebottle flew out. Miss Crawford froze.

BZZZZZZZZZZZZZZ! BZZZZZZZZZZZZZZ! BZZZZZZZZZ—

And then, with one huge leap into the air, the teacher caught the poor thing on the end of her tongue and chewed it up like a juicy sultana.

Next to join the show was Mr Sampson. Robert made him shove as many ice-cubes down his trousers as possible (two-hundred-and-seventeen in total), after which Mrs Mason danced an Irish jig in a bowl full of jelly, Mr Ahmed played the piano with his face, Miss Picardo sang a song about poo and Mrs Dillane wrote rude words up her arms with a permanent marker pen.

The school laughed their heads off throughout the whole thing, pleased Robert Williams was bullying the teachers instead of them for a change.

"And fer the grand finale," the boy announced two hours later, "Mrs Granger will paint 'er feet wiv strawberry jam then stand in a bucket of—"

The double doors to the school hall crashed open and in charged the Inspector. She was followed by a couple of large women wearing black suits and dark glasses. They were carrying an enormous television screen between the two of them.

"Questions!" cried the Inspector, marching towards the stage as her colleagues plugged in the screen. "So many questions! First, why is Mrs Granger putting her bare feet in that bucket of red ants?"

Robert shrugged.

"To raise money fer charity," he said, his boosted brain answering for him.

"Why does Mr Sampson have two-hundred-and-seventeen ice-cubes shoved down his trousers?"

"He were feelin' a bit warm," he replied.

"Why does Mrs Dillane have ******** written on her arm?"

"Inspector, mind yer language. There's Reception kiddies 'ere, ya know?"

"Why did Mr Ahmed play Chopsticks with his face?"

"Because 'is fingers woz feelin' a bit—" Robert creased his enormous forehead. "'Ere, ow d'ya know about that?"

"And lastly, are you familiar with the term, 'Live

video footage'?"

"Well, duh, it's video footage what's live, even Billy Radcliffe knows *that.* What's wiv all the questions, Inspector?"

The pint-sized woman pulled out a remote control the size of her leg and pointed it at the screen.

CLICK!

It was the most satisfying click I had ever heard.

I was going to enjoy this.

"On a weekday afternoon," the Inspector explained, "when I'm not ensuring the smooth-running of our nation's primary school education system, I like to watch *Boring Old Junk Hunt* on Channel One. But today when I turned on my set, I saw *this* instead."

She signalled towards the screen. Channel One wasn't showing its usual programmes. It was showing video footage of our school hall and all of us in it, just as we were at that very moment, *live.*

The sight of it took a moment to sink in. But gradually, one by one, the other children spotted themselves on the screen and started to look for the hidden camera. Of course they would never find it, because, 1) it was microscopic, and, 2) it was filming them from behind a fake freckle on the end of my nose.

"School inspectors en't allowed to make secret videos!" flustered Robert. "Switch it off! Switch it off!"

"It's not *me* who's filming it," snapped the Inspector, "and frankly I don't care who is. All I know is this debacle of a talent show has been shown live on TV for the past two hours, and not just on Channel One."

CLICK!

Dana Aintree jumped to her feet and gasped with horror.

"We're on Channel *Two* as well?!" she cried. "Oh my *days,* someone fetch me a *lip-gloss,* I must look *hideous* after all that laughing."

She did.

But the Inspector hadn't finished.

"That's not all," she replied. *CLICK!* "You're also on Channel Three." *CLICK!* "And Four." *CLICK!* "Five." *CLICK!* "Six." *CLICK!* "Seven." *CLICK!* "Eight." *CLICK!* "And almost twenty-nine-thousand other channels worldwide." *CLICK! CLICK! CLICK! CLICK! CLICK!*

"Twenty-nine-thousand channels?!" gaped Dana. "We're all *famous!"* Then she turned to me with disgust and the microscopic camera on the end of my nose zoomed in up her left nostril. "Except *you,* Billy

*Sad*cliffe. You're too *thick* to be famous," and a close-up of her snotty nasal hair appeared on the screen.

The Inspector marched to the front of the hall, wagging her finger in Robert Williams's red face.

"The world has been watching you," she said, crossly. "It has watched you bullying these teachers and you'll not get away with it for a second longer. Ladies, take him away."

At her command, the two large women marched onto the stage. They seized Robert Williams by the arms and lifted him up as if filled with feathers, where he kicked and shouted in protest as they carried him into the playground.

The rest of us ran outside to watch.

At the end of the netball court, there was a car. Not a regular car but a long, black limousine, with silver hubcaps and a little flag on the bonnet. That was weird. I mean, how could a school inspector afford such a fancy car?

The women put Robert inside and locked the doors.

"Show's over," announced the Inspector. "Robert Williams will be taken to a safe place where he can—"

"AAAAAAAARRRRRGH!!" That was Dana Aintree. She was staring up at the canteen roof,

clinging to the arm of the girl called Sally. "*ALIENS!* THE *ALIENS* HAVE *LANDED!*"

"Are you sure?" replied Sally, squinting up at whatever it was. "I mean, it doesn't look so much like a flying saucer as a flying *baking-tray.*"

I chuckled into my collar and Dana's face wrinkled like a prune.

"What're *you* laughing at?" she hissed.

"Oh nothing, it's just, that's not a spaceship, Dana," I said. "For a start, it doesn't have a rocket combustion chamber, a propellant turbopump or any compressed nitrogen pressuring bottles, so quite how you think it would—"

"Oh, be *quiet,* Billy!" snapped the girl. "You think you're so *clever* lately, *don't* you? Okay, *smarty-* pants, if it's not a flying *saucer,* what *is* it?"

Everyone gazed up at the corrugated iron roof of the old brick building, and there, on top of the storeroom, like a dinner-plate perched on the head of a pin, sat the most enormously colossal, the most gigantically marvellous satellite dish in the history of the world.

The playground gaped up at it as the Inspector's eyes bulged to the point of bursting.

"Questions!" she shrieked. "Too many questions! Who put a satellite dish on that roof and how will I explain it to the Board of Inspectors?!"

This was it. Time to confess. Time to tell everyone about the recipe and stop it falling into the wrong hands ever again. And the satellite dish would prove I was telling the truth.

"Me," I said, loudly. "I put it there."

The Inspector scrutinised my face.

"You?"

"Yes, I built it from various kitchen appliances. You know, toasters, blenders, that sort of thing. Then I made a microscopic camera from an electric egg timer and secretly recorded the talent show so the world could see what a big bully Robert Williams is." I picked the freckle from my nose and held it out to show her. "See? Well, I mean, you can't *actually* see because it's microscopic, but it's definitely there, I promise."

The Inspector frowned at the speck of nothingness on the end of my finger.

"This is no time for messing around, young man," she snapped. "I've had enough of you pretending you're clever to last me a lifetime."

"I'm not pretending, Inspector, it's true. The reason I was able to build that satellite dish is the same reason Robert Williams was clever enough to hypnotise the teachers. You see, there's this recipe, a recipe for a drink called Auntie Brenda's Brain Booster Juice and—"

"Sorry," the Inspector cut in, shaking her head, "are you telling me your auntie makes magic brain potions that will turn any Tom, Dick or Harry into a genius?"

"Well, she's not *my* auntie, but, yes."

"And what does your uncle do," she asked, "knit bobble hats for pixies?" As the other children laughed hysterically, the teachers came back to their senses and into the sunlight, rubbing their eyes as if having been awakened from a long and heavy sleep. "Time to go home, everyone," instructed the Inspector. "I'll be back first thing tomorrow to appoint a new head teacher."

"But Inspector, you've *got* to believe me!" I cried. "You can't let Robert Williams keep hold of that recipe! He could make another batch, or he could give it to someone even meaner than *he* is! Please, Inspector, you have to listen!"

She turned abruptly.

"Go home, Barney," she said. "I will not discuss this with you any further," and she got into the limo and closed the door.

"It's Billy!" I cried. "Billy Radcliffe! And I'm telling the truth, Inspector, please!"

But the car was already leaving the playground. My plan had failed. I'd told everyone about the Juice and no-one had believed me. And if building a giant satellite dish out of baking-trays hadn't convinced them, what on earth would?

My triple-boosted brain whirred like a well-oiled cog. Time for plan number two.

13

THE THIRD BATCH

Plan number two in my mission to stop Robert Williams using the recipe was too big for me to handle alone. But to my surprise, when I arrived home from school that day, the answer to my problem was sitting on our living room sofa, staring me right in the face.

"Andy?" I scowled. It was my brother, but he looked different to how I remembered. He was taller, spottier and his top lip was fluffy like a vacuum cleaner had exploded in his face. "Why are you out of your bedroom? Did you finally kill all the zombies?"

"Don't be silly, little bruv," he muttered, staring at his phone. "You can't kill a zombie. They're already dead."

He had a point.

"Andy," I said, "can I talk to you about something?"

My brother pulled a face like he'd just been stung by a wasp.

"Why?"

"I've got a problem and I need your help."

"It's not that rash on your bum again, is it? Cuz I can't face your butt cheeks twice in one year, Billy."

"It's not about my rash, it's about something I found in the playground this week..." and in one long breath I told him the whole story, from finding the recipe to Robert Williams being taken away by the school inspector.

Andy nodded throughout, as if I was saying something perfectly normal like what I'd had for lunch or how many outer-space dinosaurs I'd made that day.

"So," he mused, "what you're saying is, you're clever."

"For now, yes. My brain's still boosted from yesterday."

"So, if I ask you a question you'll, like, know the answer and stuff."

"That's right," I told him. "Ask me anything you want."

Andy scratched at his fuzzy chin. I could tell when my brother was thinking because his eyes rolled back in his head and his nostrils turned practically inside-out. You see, when it comes to brains, Andy is just like me (as clever as a fish is furry) and it's hard to come up with a question when you literally know nothing at all.

In the end, he typed something into the search engine of his phone instead.

"Right, little bruv," he said, "tell me something about whales."

"Whales or Wales?" I asked him.

Andy shrugged.

"What's the difference?"

"Three and a half million Welsh people."

Andy did his thinking face again.

"What've three and a half million Welsh people got to do with a giant fish?" he asked.

"You mean whales with an H," I told him, "but they're not a type of fish, Andy, they're a type of mammal known as cetaceans. There are seventy-seven species of cetaceans, all of which can be split into two groups: the baleen whales and the toothed whales. The biggest species is the Blue Whale or Balaenoptera musculus, which grows as heavy as a hundred and fifty tonnes. An example of a smaller species is the Minke Whale or Balaenoptera acutorostrata, which is only ten tonnes at its largest but can swim up to—"

"All right, all right, I said tell me *something* about whales, Billy, not tell me *everything* about whales. No-one likes a show-off."

"Sorry. It's difficult to stop once I get going. It's like the Juice takes over my brain. Hey, maybe I should go on 'Who Wants to be a Gazillionaire?'," I chuckled.

Andy's eyes flashed like a couple of pound signs.

"*That* is a wicked idea," he grinned.

"*That* was a joke," I replied. "I've had enough of being on TV to last me a lifetime, thanks."

"Fair enough," he said. "But you don't have to go on the telly to get rich now you're a genius. You could invent something instead. Like…a mobile phone that's also a dishwasher!"

"You'd need very small plates," I told him.

"Or a very *big* phone," he replied, hopefully.

"Andy, we're not using the Juice to make money, it's not right. We should give the recipe to someone in authority so they can contact the world's greatest scientists, who'll use their boosted intelligence to cure diseases, stop climate change and end poverty. *That's* why I told you about it, Andy, so you can help me convince the Inspector that the Brain Booster Juice is real before Robert Williams does something awful with his copy of the recipe."

"Like what?"

"I dunno, like making a huge batch of Juice and

selling it on the internet."

The pound signs in Andy's eyes turned to diamonds.

"*That* is a wicked idea," he said. I gave him my most unimpressed face, the same one mum gave me when I interrupted her poker game, and he folded his arms in a sulk. "Fine. But at least let me have a swig before you go giving it away for nothing."

"Oh, well, I dunno, Andy…"

"I won't help with your plan if you don't."

"Hey, that's not fair. I'm just trying to do the right thing and get the recipe into safe hands. If I go around giving it to everyone who asks for it, the Juice could cause even more trouble than it already has."

"I'm not everyone, Billy. I'm me, stupid Andy Radcliffe, and there's this girl at school who I really like. But girls like Sarah don't give idiots like me a second look."

"Andy, you shouldn't change who you are just to please someone else." It was like I was the pot, he was the kettle and here I was telling him we were both the same colour. "I mean, if this girl doesn't like you for who you are then that's her tough—" *CHING!* "Sorry, what did you say her name was?"

"Sarah."

"Is she friends with the girl who works in The

Next-Door Shop?"

Andy crumpled his nose.

"Yeah. How'd you know that?"

A marvellous idea formed in my boosted brain.

"Oh, the shop girl and me are really good friends," I lied, knowing Sarah already liked Andy as much as he liked her (the poor, deranged girl). "I can get you a date with Sarah. You won't need any Brain Booster Juice, but you have to help with my plan first. Deal?"

Andy smiled.

"Deal," he agreed.

We woke up early the next day to get to school before anyone else. Mrs Granger was usually the first person to arrive, so she could throw things at everyone else as they walked past her classroom window, but the only person who'd been here today was the milkman. He'd left ten crates of half-pint cartons behind the canteen for our breaktime drink, not realising they would be part of a genius plan to reveal Auntie Brenda's Brain Booster Juice to the whole world.

Well, to the school inspector at least.

"I hated milk-time when I came here," remarked Andy, as we climbed over a fence and made our way round to the back of the building. "It was all thick and sour and gross."

I placed down my bag full of Brain Booster Juice bottles next to the crates.

"You'd like it today," I told him. "Did you bring the funnel and the glue-stick?"

Carefully, I peeled apart the top of our first carton.

"Billy, are you sure this is a good idea? I mean, this plan of yours, it's a bit, you know, mad and that."

"Desperate times call for desperate measures," I said. "Come on, hold the carton open, we haven't got long before the teachers arrive." He did as I asked and I dripped a dollop of Brain Booster Juice into the milk. This third batch was much thicker than the others because I hadn't added the milk until now. It sunk to the bottom of the carton like a stone. "Okay, now stick the top back together and give it a good shake while I open the next one."

We worked fast, and soon we had re-sealed our one hundred-and-twenty-fourth carton. To the innocent bystander the ten crates of milk looked as ordinary as...well, ten crates of milk. But to me they were one-hundred-and-twenty-four glorious cartons of Auntie Brenda's Brain Booster Juice, all ready and waiting for the teachers to hand out to every pupil that very morning.

And *what* a morning it would be!

14

MILK-TIME

"Mrs Granger!" cried Joseph Compton, frantically scrubbing his tongue on his sleeve. "A mouse has pooed in my milk! It's stuck in the straw, Mrs Granger, look!"

The teacher peered down the straw at the alleged poo and a crab-eye peered back up at *her*.

"Brainless child," she muttered, "that's not a mouse dropping, that's a raisin. The dairy must be trying out a healthier milk with fruit in it because Mr Sampson had one in his coffee this morning. Suck it up, boy, it's one of your five a day."

That was all the encouragement he needed. And when every last drop had been guzzled and all of the cartons were empty, I waited for the fun to begin.

"Cake-holes shut, lug-holes open," demanded Mrs Granger after lunch. She placed a mug of sugary, black coffee down on her desk. "This afternoon we'll be learning about a famous author. Someone tell the morons on the Wally Table what an author is," and she pointed a talon at Peter Giselle.

"An author is someone who writes books, Mrs Granger," he replied.

She turned again to the Wally Table.

"And a *book,* for those of you too intrinsically thick to know it," she said, "is one of those paper things we keep in the library. Right then, who's heard of Charles Dickens?"

"Me," smiled Joseph Compton.

The teacher screwed up her face as if she'd just stood in something a dog had done on the pavement.

"You have not," she told him.

"I have too," he replied. "Charles Dickens was an English author, born on February 7th 1812."

Mrs Granger snorted.

"Huh, read that in a cracker, did you?"

"No," he replied, a little confused by her reaction. "Crackers have jokes in them, Mrs Granger, not facts. February 7th 1812 was a Friday and the baby Charles was delivered at a quarter past six in the morning."

"I'll give you a quarter past my stapler if you don't stop rabbiting on," she snarled. "Now, who can tell me one of—"

Dana Aintree's hand shot into the air so fast her backside left the chair.

"The *Pickwick* Papers!" she shouted.

"Dana What's-Your-Face," snapped the teacher, "I haven't finished the question, so pipe down before I throw something at you. Now, who can tell me one of—"

"Oliver Twist!" cried Mandy Langton.

"Mandy Long-Tongue, I *said,* I haven't finished the—"

"Nicholas Nickleby!" yelled Joseph.

"I haven't—"

"The Old Curiosity Shop!"

"You don't even—"

"Barnaby Rudge!"

"Can you just—"

"Martin Chuzzlewit!"

"STOP! STOP! STOP!" Mrs Granger took a huge swig of her coffee. "Right, that's it, I won't ask the question at all if you're going to keep interrupting me."

But we didn't care if she asked it or not. We already knew what the question was and the titles of Charles Dickens's books were now flying in thick and fast from every direction.

"Dombey and Son!"

"David Copperfield!"

"Bleak House!"

"Hard Times!"

"Little Dorrit!"

"A Tale of Two Cities!"

"Great Expectations!"

"Our Mutual Friend!"

"The Mystery of Edwin Drood!"

We even listed them in the order they were written.

"Aha!" shouted the teacher. A wild expression of joy flashed over her face. "You missed some out! You're all *stupid!*" and she leaned in to blow a big, wet raspberry in Dana Aintree's face.

"Actually, Mrs Granger," I said, with as much respect as I could muster for the miserable old witch, "I believe I know the titles you're referring to and there's a reason we didn't list them."

"Barney No-Brain," she growled, "have you been reading my notes again?"

"For example, Dickens wrote a set of works entitled Sketches by Boz," I told her, "first published in 1836. We didn't add it to our list, Mrs Granger, because we thought you were asking about Dickins's *novels,* whereas Sketches by Boz is a collection of shorter pieces. However, if you literally want to know *everything* Charles Dickens ever wrote, we could always start again."

The teacher drew in a huge lungful of air, hoping

she'd suck me into her mouth so she could spit me out of the window.

"That will *not* be necessary," she rumbled.

Joseph Compton stood up.

"Good decision, Mrs Granger," he said, seriously. "I mean, don't get me wrong, Dickens was a great writer, but I much prefer the works of Geoffrey Chaucer." Mutterings of, *Me too*, and, *Hear, hear*, echoed around the room. Mrs Granger swallowed the rest of her coffee in one gulp. "Chaucer lived from 1342 to 1400. He wrote the Canterbury Tales, a collection of stories told by various pilgrims as they travel from London to Canterbury."

"Blah, blah, blah, Mr Wotsit," scoffed the teacher. "Nobody cares."

"Actually, Mrs Granger, there are quite a few English literature scholars who care very much," said Joseph. "Did you know that each story in the Canterbury Tales has its own title? The first one is The Knight's Tale."

A bolt of electricity seemed to shoot up the legs of Dana Aintree's chair and she hurdled the Vaguely Clever Table, landing with both hands flat on the teacher's desk.

"The Miller's Tale!" she bellowed at a totally

unimpressed Mrs Granger.

The rest of the class joined in too.

"The Reeve's Tale!"

"The Cook's Tale!"

"The Wife of Bath's Tale!"

"The Friar's Tale!"

"The Man of Law's Tale!"

"STOP IT RIGHT NOW!" Mrs Granger clutched at her hair with both hands. "HOW *DARE* YOU LIST THE CANTERBURY TALES WITHOUT MY PERMISSION?!"

"Because they're a highly notable piece of English literature, Mrs Granger," frowned Joseph. There was simply no stopping him – it was marvellous to watch. "Of course, Chaucer is also much admired for his poetic works, like: *After the death of Tholomee the king, That al Egipte hadde in his governing, Regned his queen Cleopataras, Til on a tyme befell ther swiche a cas—"*

"WHY ARE YOU TALKING GOBBLEDYGOOK?!" shrieked the teacher.

"It's not gobbledygook, Mrs Granger, it's Middle English," explained Joseph. "The dialects of Middle English can vary depending on the time and place in which they were spoken, which, in contrast to Old and Modern English, is quite an interesting phenomenon because it's the only—"

CRASH!

That was the sound of Mrs Granger knocking over a bookcase as she blasted out of the classroom door like a cork from a bottle.

The room fell silent, everyone baffled by the teacher's strange behaviour.

"Oh *dear,*" remarked Dana, "Mrs Granger must be *unwell* and it's against the school *rules* for us to be in a *room* without a *teacher*. Let's all go to Mr *Sampson's* class until she feels *better,*" and she was so busy blabbering on about Pythagoras's Theorem as we headed along the corridor, she forgot to splatter me with her sparkly lip-gloss.

"Ah good, reinforcements," sang Mr Sampson when we entered the room, without so much as an *ARGH!* It was the first time I'd seen him without his parrot or his eye-patch. "Come on in, 5G, we're having a science lesson." The room was jam-packed with test tubes containing various liquids, all bubbling and steaming over rows of Bunsen burners. Colin Bradley had a magnifying glass strapped to his head. He was carefully prodding at something with a knife. "Over here, Billy," called the teacher. "Take a look at Colin's experiment."

Peering through the magnifying glass, I saw

what appeared to be an incredibly small fried egg.

"Is that what I think it is?" I gaped.

"Yep," beamed Colin. "Half an atom. I split it myself. I mean, I know the atom has been split before, Billy, but I'm fairly sure this is the first time a class of ten and eleven-year-old children has done it."

"You mean you've *all* split an atom?"

"Of course," replied Mr Sampson. "But young Colin here is the only one who's cut it *directly* down the middle. Now, see if you can cut that half into quarters, Colin."

There was a knock on the classroom door. The Inspector had arrived and Mrs Granger was with her. The little woman was standing in the doorway with her mouth hanging open, whilst Mrs Granger clung to the wall like either she or it was about to fall down.

"Ah, Inspector, welcome back," chirped Mr Sampson. "We're splitting atoms. Would you care to join us?"

The Inspector aimed her trembling eyeballs in my direction.

"Some questions for you, Barney," she said, as the rest of my class joined in with the experiments. I left Colin slicing up his atom like a tiny pizza and joined her in the doorway. "Firstly, how did the Year 1 class compose a fourth movement to Mozart's

Piano Concerto Number 6 in B-flat Major on a plastic xylophone?"

"Well, I expect they hit it with those little wooden sticks," I told her.

Mrs Granger clung tighter still to the wall.

"Second question," the Inspector went on. "Why are the Reception children currently outside re-enacting the Battle of Trafalgar with perfectly-formed, life-sized figures of the British and French troops they've sculpted from salt-dough?"

"Erm, because they ran out of plasticine?" I suggested.

"And finally, have I *really* just witnessed a Year 3 class disrupting the space-time continuum with a junk-modelled teleportation machine they made out of an old shoe-box, three toilet-roll tubes and a coat-hanger?"

"You might've done," I said. "Did it work?"

"Well, they've just teleported the school rabbit out of its cage and onto Mrs Granger's lap, so I presume so, yes."

Mrs Granger slid down the wall. The Inspector hauled her back up with impatience, took the stapler out of her cardigan pocket, placed it against the collar of her pink floral dress and…

PING!

…stapled her to the door-frame, where she hung like an oversized sack on a very small hook. The Inspector beckoned me closer then stood on a chair to whisper into my ear.

"Billy Radcliffe," she said, "I have a few questions about this brain recipe of yours. Headmaster's office, *now*.

15

DOUBLE TROUBLE

The Inspector paced the floor of the headmaster's office like a police detective, whilst Mrs Granger ate coffee granules from the jar with a spoon.

"I told you yesterday about the recipe," I said, "but you wouldn't believe me. So I made a stronger version of the Brain Booster Juice and mixed it into the school milk this morning."

"Like an undiluted orange squash," Mrs Granger giggled. She had never giggled before. But then she had never eaten her weekly allowance of caffeine in thirty seconds before either. "I love squash."

"Yes, it was a bit like undiluted squash," I said, "like a...like a..." but I couldn't think of the word for it.

"Concentrate," said the Inspector.

"I am concentrating," I told her, "I just can't think the word for it."

Mrs Granger snorted and a shower of coffee

sprayed out of her nose.

"Concentrate," the Inspector explained, "is the word we use for a stronger version of something, Billy. I thought you were meant to be clever now."

"I was, but my Brain Booster's wearing off. Anyway, I don't like being clever. I thought being a super-genius would stop other people being bullies, but it didn't. All I want is to give the recipe to someone who'll keep it safe, so it can't cause any more trouble."

The Inspector held out a baby-sized hand.

"Very well," she said. "Hand it over."

"Erm," I replied, (this was awkward), "no offence, Inspector, but I meant someone a bit, you know, *higher up* than you."

The tiny woman pulled her head into her neck like a startled turtle.

"What's *that* supposed to mean?"

"Oh no, I don't mean *physically* higher up than you, Inspector. What I mean is, it should go to the highest authority, like, I don't know, the Queen or someone."

"I spy a little silhouettoo of a ham!" sang Mrs Granger. "I love Freddie."

The Inspector took her spoon so she couldn't eat any more coffee.

"If it's someone of importance you want," said the woman, "then someone of importance you shall have. Mrs Granger, pass me the telephone – I'm going to call the Prime Minister."

Mrs Granger guffawed in her face. A splattering of soggy coffee granules spattered all over her glasses and stuck there like mud.

"It's not like ordering a pizza, you know," the teacher chuckled. "You can't just call Dial-a-Prime-Minister and ask for a stuffed-crust leader of the nation with a side order of cabinet ministers." She sighed wistfully. "I love politicians." And then she thought about that for a moment. "No, wait, actually I don't."

The Inspector positioned a small filing cabinet near Mrs Granger's feet, pulled out three of the drawers and climbed up it like a ladder. Then she stood on the top and stared the teacher square in the eye.

"For your information," she said, her face stony, "the Prime Minister and I spoke only yesterday. He saw Robert Williams on the television and realised a boy with his intellect would be a huge asset to the British government. So he asked me to bring him to Downing Street."

"*That's* why you put him in that big car," I

realised.

"Yes, and when we got there, he told the Prime Minister about the recipe straight away. However, the silly boy thought the effects of the Juice would last forever, so he had *eaten* his copy in the back of the limousine to make sure no-one else was as clever as him. Ten minutes later, he was back to being his usual stupid self."

"Ah," smiled Mrs Granger, blissfully, "I love irony."

"So, you see," the Inspector went on, "that's why the Prime Minister needs *your* copy of the Brain Booster recipe. I mean, I'd rather not have to call Number 10 and have you taken away too, Billy, but if you won't hand it over I'm afraid you leave me no choice."

The Inspector lifted the receiver.

"It's all right," I said, taking the recipe from my pocket, "you don't need to call the Prime Minister – this is exactly what I wanted, for the recipe to be in safe hands."

I held out the page. The Inspector snatched it like a precious jewel and then hugged it like a long-lost friend.

"RESULT!" she shouted, kissing the paper. "GET IN! BACK OF THE NET!"

"Erm, why has that made you so happy?" I asked. "You *were* telling the truth about giving it to the Prime Minister, weren't you, Inspector?"

"Too flamin' right!" she beamed. "The PM said whoever gets him *your* copy of the recipe will be rewarded with two million pounds. *Two million!* I'll never have to work again! No more smelly old schools! No more horrid children! No more useless teachers!"

"Hey, that's not fair," I said. "It's *my* recipe, not yours. Why should *you* end up being a millionaire? In fact, why should *anyone* end up being a millionaire? You're as bad as my brother," I told her, "but at least he's got the excuse of being fourteen years old and as thick as custard."

Mrs Granger tried to nudge the Inspector but forgot about the height difference and elbowed her in the face.

"You know what you should do, Inspector?" she said in a loud whisper, tipping the last of the coffee grains into her mouth. "Make a copy of the recipe before giving it to the Prime Minister. That way, you'll be a millionaire *and* a genius."

"Mrs Granger!" I cried. "You see, this is *exactly* why I want the recipe in safe hands – so people like *you* can't get hold of it!"

"Well, I think it's an excellent idea," the Inspector grinned, and she unfolded the paper. But then she stopped smiling and held the recipe up to the light, squinting at something near the bottom of the page. "A question," she said. "Why is there a hole at the end of this list?"

Of course – the tomato stain!

Marvellous!

"Oh, that's where the final ingredient was," I told her, "and before you ask, no, I *won't* tell you what it is and I *never* will because you're both *horrible* and neither one of you *deserve* that recipe!" and with that, I stormed out of the office in a flush of anger, slamming the door behind me.

My stomach filled with butterflies, but soon it grew stronger and less throwy-up, as if my body was a dandelion stalk turning into the magnificent trunk of an ancient oak tree.

Yes, it was amazing to have won that small battle. But how long would it take the two awful women to realise I'd mixed the Brain Booster Juice with one-hundred-and-twenty-four cartons of the missing ingredient that very morning?

16

NUMBER 10

The following day was a Saturday. I woke early and was just getting dressed when Andy came into my bedroom with the phone in his hand.

"Billy boy," he said, "there's call for you. It's some posh woman."

I didn't know any posh women. But I took the phone anyway and held it up to my ear.

"This is the Prime Minister's secretary," said a voice. My mouth went dry, as if someone had stuffed a wad of toilet-paper in there. "The Prime Minister requests your presence at Number 10 as a matter of some urgency."

"Who is it?" whispered Andy.

"It's the Prime Minister's secretary," I hissed back at him. "She wants my presents. Have we got any presents?"

"Not your *presents,*" the posh woman told me, "your *presence,*" which was exactly what I had said.

"A car will arrive shortly to collect you. See you soon, Billy," and she hung up the phone.

Andy looked at me and I looked at Andy.

"Do you think it's about the recipe?" I asked him. "Do you think the Inspector's told him about the missing ingredient?"

"I expect so," he said. "Unless the Prime Minister wants to discuss next year's projected economic growth climate with you," and he chuckled at whatever that was he'd just said.

I narrowed my eyes.

"What are you talking about?"

"My educated supposition," he said, "is the Inspector has developed a mental scotoma to the fact you mixed the Brain Booster Juice with *milk* yesterday, thus rendering her unable to deduce the identity of the missing ingredient and compelling her to relinquish the recipe to the Prime Minister, who in turn has summoned you to Downing Street in the hope you may disclose the desired information to the government of this land."

I looked carefully at Andy's face.

"You took one of those milk cartons yesterday, didn't you?"

"Might've done," he said. "But what I mean is, the Inspector must've been too stupid to figure out the missing ingredient and now the Prime Minister wants to know what it is. Did I say, 'thus'?"

"Yes, you did."

"Wicked."

A car horn sounded outside the house and both of us ran to the window. It was the same black limousine that had taken Robert Williams to Downing Street.

"Should I go?" I asked Andy.

My brother shrugged.

"Better check with Mum, I suppose."

Running downstairs two steps at a time, I found Mum in the kitchen as usual. Her weekend poker tournament was already in full-swing.

"Mum," I said, knocking politely on the door, "this might sound a bit weird and that, but...can I go to Downing Street to visit the Prime Minister?"

"Full house!" she yelled.

And I took that as a yes.

The driver of the limo was a stern-looking woman in a black suit and dark glasses. Her chin was square like a brick and she said nothing at all until we reached Downing Street, where she went, "Nrrrgh," and pointed at the big, shiny, black door of Number 10.

A policeman was standing in front of it. He showed me inside and took me into a small office, where a lady was busy working at an old-fashioned desk with a huge pile of paperwork in front of her.

"Ah," she smiled, looking up from her work as I entered the room, "you must be Billy." It was the posh woman from the telephone. "Thanks for coming in at such short notice."

"That's all right," I said. "But I'm afraid I don't have any presents for you."

She gave another smile and pressed a buzzer on her desk.

BZZZZZZ!

A man's voice came out of a small speaker.

"Yes?"

"Billy Radcliffe here to see you, sir."

"Excellent. Send him in, Miss Fletcher. Not a moment to lose."

BZZZZZZ!

She signalled to a large wooden door with a brass handle. It was so heavy I needed both hands to pull it open and when I entered the room I came face to face with *the Prime Minister himself.* I recognised him from the telly but he wasn't scary at all. He was just a regular man in a very big suit, with a tie that looked like wallpaper, who was squirming around as if swarms of ants were running marathons inside his trouser-legs.

"Excuse the wriggling," he said. "Can't keep still when there something urgent to be done. Bit of a global emergency, I'm afraid. Won't say what it is just yet, Billy, but all will become clear in good time. I suppose you know why I've brought you here."

He held up my copy of the Brain Booster recipe.

"Yes, sir. You want to know what the missing ingredient is."

"Correction," he said, hopping from one foot to the other, "I *need* to know what the missing ingredient is, Billy. I've had my top scientist trying to work out what's missing since last night, but he's drawn a blank every time."

CRASH!

The large wooden door with the big brass handle was thrown open by a man in a white lab coat.

"Prime Minister!" puffed the man, running into the room. "There's been another accident with the Juice experiments!"

"Professor Higgins, please tell me you haven't made *another* batch. I thought we agreed you would *stop* trying to guess the missing ingredient until I'd spoken with Billy."

"I know, I know, but I had an idea, sir. It was a

genius idea, an absolutely genius idea." He paused. "Well, I *thought* it was an absolutely genius idea, but it turned out to be rather a rubbish one, I'm afraid, sir."

The Prime Minister leapt into the air like an Irish dancer.

"What did you put in it *this* time?" he asked, desperately.

Professor Higgins cringed, as if he had done something terrible (which he had).

"Frogspawn," he said, blushing.

The Prime Minister laughed.

"Sorry, Professor," he chuckled, "for a second there I thought you said frogspawn, when what you *actually* said was…?"

"Erm, frogspawn," the professor repeated.

"*What?!*" yelled the Prime Minister. "That's not even a food!"

"I thought it was in keeping with the fish theme," whined the professor. "You know, crab-eyes, pickled eels, frogspawn? And by the time I realised frogs aren't fish, it was too late – he'd drank the whole jugful."

"Who had, Professor? Who drank this terrible concoction of yours?"

"Erm, William," he muttered so quietly we could

hardly hear him at all.

The Prime Minister frowned.

"William? I don't know anyone called William."

"No, sir, not William." The professor gulped. "*Williams,* sir. As in, Robert Williams."

"*WHAT?!*" The Prime Minister bounced on the spot like his legs were made out of rubber, his arms flapping about at his sides. "You were meant to send the boy home, Professor, not feed him one of your crazy experiments!"

"I thought he'd remember the missing ingredient if I kept him here long enough, sir, but I'm afraid he didn't. He volunteered to take part in the experiment though, sir, really he did, and he's only experienced one tiny little side-effect."

BOOM!

The noise came from the corridor outside. It shook the floor like an earthquake.

BOOM!

"*How* tiny?" asked the Prime Minister.

BOOM!

An oil painting of the Queen fell off the wall.

BOOM!

"Well, quite a big sort of tiny, I suppose," the professor confessed.

BOOM!

The sound was getting closer.

BOOM!

And between the thuds came the sound of moving liquid.

BOOM!

Like a giant hot water bottle was marching through Number 10.

BOOM!

Heading straight towards us.

BOOM!

Until…

BOOM!

An enormous leg stomped into the open doorway like a big, fat, wobbly sausage, bringing with it the enormous, quivering, jellylike body of Robert Williams.

"What in the name of sanity…?" breathed the Prime Minister, gawping up at the boy. "Professor Higgins, *look* at him!"

It was impossible *not* to look at him. He was taking up most of the doorway.

Robert's stomach bulged from the top of his trousers like an over-inflated beachball. His face was swollen and his skin was see-through – yes, *completely see-through!* – so we could wave to the horrified Miss Fletcher through his head.

"He's a bit bloated," the Professor explained, "and his skin's a little translucent but—"

"A bit bloated?!" shrieked the Prime Minister, now shaking like a pneumatic drill. *"A little translucent?!* You've turned him to jelly, Professor Higgins!"

"No, sir, not jelly," the professor corrected. "Don't you see those hundreds of little black dots all wriggling around inside of him? He's frogspawn, sir."

"Blook blot blee's blun bloo blee!" spluttered Robert, his head wobbling like a blancmange as he spoke. "Blust bloo blait blil bli blell bly blad!"

We couldn't understand what he said, but it wasn't a happy splutter.

"We can't send him home like this," sobbed the Prime Minister. "How long until he's back to normal, Professor?"

"Ah," said the man, "now, the other volunteers are still showing a few side-effects, so, based on my current hypothesis, taking everything into account and considering all potential outcomes, I remain open-minded to any eventuality."

The Prime Minister had no strength left to move and instead collapsed heavily into his chair.

"And what's *that* supposed to mean?" he asked,

wearily.

"It means, erm, I have no idea how long it will take, sir. Sorry."

The Prime Minister pulled himself up and gave me a serious look.

"Billy," he said, "it seems that little global emergency isn't the only reason we need your recipe – we have to boost someone's brain so they're clever enough to reverse the professor's experiments."

"Yes, sir," I replied, a little shyly, "but the thing is, if you give the Juice to the wrong person it can cause even more trouble, like it did when Robert Williams got hold of the recipe. *That's* why I wouldn't tell the Inspector what the missing ingredient is and *that's* why I'd like to keep it a secret, sir. If I can."

"I understand, Billy, I understand. And I think I have an idea." He stood up with renewed energy. "But first you must see what we're dealing with here, so you can make an informed decision. Professor, show Billy the other victims of your Juice experiments and fast, before those tadpoles turn into frogs and make a horrible mess on the floor."

"Bli blon't blant blo blurn blinto blogs!" spluttered Robert Williams, and as we left the room, Miss Fletcher threw a bucket of water over him so he didn't dry out.

17

THE FRUIT AND VEG CABINET

Professor Higgins took us to a small room, where four people were drinking coffee.

The first one was sitting directly opposite the door. She was reading a newspaper, but as we walked in the pages were lowered and an eerie porcelain face appeared from behind it. Her skin was cracked like broken ice and something egg-shaped was growing from the middle of her forehead. The bump grew bigger and bigger, until it had swelled to the size of a large pebble, and then – *CRACK!* – it burst open and a thick, yellow yolk ran down the bridge of her nose before plopping onto her dress.

To her left, an incredibly tall man with bright green skin was sipping tea. He wasn't tall like a basketball player, but tall like a lamppost and just as thin, as if two people had taken hold of him at either end and stretched him out like an uncooked pizza base. He looked like very long, very miserable blade of grass.

The woman next to him was short in comparison but much wider. Her arms and legs had been swallowed up by her plump body, so that only her hands and feet were now sticking out from the appropriate places. Her skin was wrinkled and sticky like a toffee-covered walnut, and she opened her lips with a gummy – *PWUCK!* – to blow a raspberry at the professor.

And lastly, on the far side of the room, was a man with fuzzy skin and a stalk coming out of his head. There was an orange crease down the middle of his face, making him look more like a hairy bottom than a person.

"Billy, these are the four most important members of my cabinet," began the Prime Minister, "or at least they *were* before the professor turned them into a shopping list. Professor Higgins, tell Billy what happened to them."

The four peculiar-looking people glowered fiercely at the professor.

"W-well," he began, nervously, "yesterday, when the Inspector brought the Brain Booster recipe to Downing Street, I conducted a series of experiments in order to discover the missing ingredient. My first idea was eggs." A second egg bulged from the chin of the porcelain-faced woman before exploding into a gunky mess down her front. "Everything has eggs in it, right?"

"No, everything does *not* have eggs in it," she snapped. An eggy stink filled the room as she spoke. "I'm really unhappy about this, Prime Minister. I'm the Chancellor of the Exchequer, for goodness sake, not the Easter Bunny."

The green man giggled.

"Chancellor of the Egg-chequer," he laughed. "That's hilarious."

"You think that's *funny*, do you?" barked the egg-woman. "At least I don't look like something a toddler wiped on his sleeve."

"Anyway," the Professor cut in, "next I wondered if prunes might be it. They're good for you, prunes, isn't that what they say? They keep you nice and regular."

"*PWUCK!* Regular?" crowed the sticky woman. "*PWUCK!* There's nothing *regular* about me. *PWUCK!* I'm a big, dried-up piece of old fruit."

"Nothing new there then," muttered the fuzzy-faced one with a smirk.

The prune woman tried to wallop him with her handbag, but she was stuck to her seat like treacle to a spoon.

"*PWUCK!* And everything's *peachy* with you, I suppose? *PWUCK!* At least I still have my own teeth."

The man snarled, showing a full set of wooden gnashers, each one covered in little grooves like the stone of a fruit.

"Is it my fault that *idiot* thought a peach was the missing ingredient?" he cried, his teeth knocking together like two coconut shells. "I'll never be able to hold my head high in parliament ever again."

The incredibly tall man whipped his head across the room like a streak of green lightning. His nose stopped only a fraction away from the peach man's face.

"Is that meant to be funny?" he snarled. "At least you can *choose* whether or not to hold your head high, Peter. Some of us can't even stand up without making a hole in the ceiling." He lashed his face across to the other side of the room and peered down at the professor. "*Let's try runner beans,* you said. *What harm can it do?* you said. *I have some left over from yesterday's dinner,* you said, *we'd might as well use them up,* you said. I have a good mind to walk out of here right now and consult my solicitor."

"Any experiments that go on inside these four walls are top secret," the Prime Minister told him, "so *no-one* will be consulting *anyone* without my permission."

"*PWUCK!* What are we expected to do then, Prime Minister? *PWUCK!* Sit around drinking coffee until our best-before dates run out?"

"Of course not," he said. "Young Billy here knows what the missing ingredient is. He's going to drink the Brain Booster Juice and cure the lot of you."

"*Me,* Prime Minister?" I gaped.

"Yes, Billy, you. We don't know how the Juice will affect other people, but we *do* know how *you* react to it. And you won't have to tell anyone the missing ingredient – only *you* will make the Juice, and only *you* will drink it. Does that sound okay, Billy?"

"I suppose so, sir, if you think I'm up to it."

"Of course you're up to it," he said, cheerfully. "But this lot can wait. First you must use your boosted brain to save the world."

"Save the…save the *world,* sir?"

"Yes, Billy, the global emergency, remember? Come along now. I'll tell you all about it on our way to the basement," and he trotted out of the room as if we were off for a stroll in the park – this morning my Brain Booster journey had been over, and now it was about to go rocketing out of this world.

18

THE FOURTH BATCH

The Prime Minister and I went downstairs to a big science laboratory in the cellar to the basement of Number 10 Downing Street (that's the secret floor *below* the basement, in case you were wondering). Laid out on a table were enough Brain Booster ingredients to turn the whole country into neuro-surgeons. But that wasn't all. The shelves of the room looked like a big supermarket, with every food item you could ever wish to find.

"I had all this delivered yesterday," the Prime Minister explained, "so Professor Higgins could conduct his experiments. You'll be able to select your missing ingredient without telling me what it is. Unless it's something really unusual and it's not here, in which case—"

"Don't worry, sir." There was a large bottle of milk between the carrots and the coconuts. "I can see it."

The Prime Minister fetched a big pot, one that looked like a witch's cauldron, and placed it down on the table.

"I'll leave you alone to make the Juice, Billy. Just make as much as you can with what you have and give me a shout when you're ready. I'll be waiting outside the door."

When the Prime Minister had gone, I put all the ingredients into the cauldron and stirred them well. Soon a familiar stench watered my eyes. There was more Brain Booster here than I'd given to the *entire school* in yesterday's milk.

The Prime Minister re-entered the room.

"Okay, Billy," he said, handing me a straw, "you start drinking and I'll tell you all about the emergency. Oh, and you'll need to swallow every last drop, I'm afraid – this is going to be quite a task." The Prime Minister's face grew more serious than bubonic plague. "Billy, last week our country received a digitally transmitted message from an unknown location."

"What, like a voicemail?" I frowned.

"Well, sort of," replied the Prime Minister.

"And you don't know who sent it?"

The Prime Minister shook his head.

"Not exactly. But we *do* know it came from somewhere on the other side of the universe."

A crab-eye shot out of my mouth and hit the

Prime Minister in the face.

"Sir," I said, "are you telling me there's another terrestrial planet with sufficient quantities of carbon and water to enable a species of intelligent living organisms to evolve?" (It seemed the quicker the Brain Booster was gulped, the quicker the Brain Booster worked.)

"That's right, Billy – *aliens* have contacted our planet and we have no idea what they're saying. It might be, *Do you mind if we pop down to Earth for a nice cup of tea and a slice of cake?* Or it could be, *Do you mind if we pop down to Earth and annihilate your species?* I've had string of language experts listening to it, but they're all baffled. You're our only hope now, Billy – the future of our world is in your hands."

I nodded seriously, because, well, this was serious. In fact it was the most seriously serious thing I had ever heard. I should say something clever, something to put the Prime Minister's mind at rest, something to reassure him there was nothing to worry about, but the last word of his sentence was flying around in my head like a bee in a jam-jar and I couldn't think of anything else.

HANDS, HANDS, HANDS, HANDS, HANDS, HANDS…

"Of course, when I saw Robert Williams on TV,"

the Prime Minister went on, "I thought he could help. That's why I had him brought here to Downing Street. But of course, he couldn't."

HANDS, HANDS, HANDS, HANDS, HANDS, HANDS…

"And then I thought, if Professor Higgins can just work out the missing ingredient, we'll be able to boost someone's brain and *they* can translate the message. But that didn't work either."

HANDS, HANDS, HANDS, HANDS, HANDS, HANDS…

My head felt as if it would burst. Like there was so much information in there, some of it had to escape.

"Billy," the Prime Minister said, "you look flushed. Can I get you a glass of water or some—"

"HANDS!" I shouted.

"Sorry?"

"BONES OF THE HUMAN HAND!" and then, in one long breath, the information poured out of my brain like water from an overflowing bathtub. "Scaphoid! Lunate! Triquetral! Pisiform! Trapezium! Trapezoid! Capitate! Hamate! Metacarpals! Proximal phalanges! Intermediate phalanges! Distal phalanges!"

GASP!

The Prime Minister was confused.

"Billy, what was that all about? Are you okay?"

"It's the Brain Booster," I told him, "I've never drank even *half* as much of it before. But I'm all right now. Let's just get on with the translation before the Juice starts to wear off."

The Prime Minister nodded and then turned to the entrance of the laboratory.

"Mrs Du Monde," he called, "you can come in now!" and the door clicked open. A slim, gappy-toothed woman trotted into the room. She was wearing a pair of wooden clogs and a beret. "Billy, this is Mrs Du Monde. Mrs Du Monde is the best language expert in the country. She's here to assist with the translation."

"Hallo!" sang the woman, in the strongest German accent I had ever heard. "Mein name ist Mrs Du Monde. Sehr gut to meet you, Billy Radcliffe."

"Guten Tag," I said, which meant, *Good day*. "Mein Gehirn ist so groß wie eine Melone und es tut weh," which meant, *My brain is the size of a melon and it hurts.*

The woman pulled her top lip up over her gums. It might've been a smile.

"Das ist gut," she said, uncertainly. "You vould like to listen to de alien message now, Billy, ja?"

"Yes, please," I replied.

Mrs Du Monde signalled to the Prime Minister and with the press of a button an unusual noise came out of the overhead speakers. It sounded like three dolphins with throat infections.

"Oo la la!" cried Mrs Du Monde, in her best French accent. "Izn't ziss zee strangest thing you 'ave ever 'eard?"

Why had she gone from German to French?

"This, erm, recording's a bit fuzzy," I said, trying to ignore her accent. "Is it the only one you have?"

"Oh, it's not a recording," replied the Prime Minister. "This message is being sent to us live from space. The aliens have been talking non-stop for over a week now."

"They're literally talking to us *right now?*" I gasped. "Wow, sir, that's incredible."

"Och, Billy me lad," tutted Mrs Du Monde, "I cannae believe you're callin' the Prime Minister a liar, ye cheeky young haggis."

"What? No, I wasn't calling him a liar, Mrs Du Monde, I was just saying—"

"By Jove, Master Radcliffe, I know precisely what you were saying and one must really learn to respect one's elders. Especially those who are thoroughly spiffing like the Prime Minister. I'm owf to spend a penny now. Back in a jiffy. Toodle pip," and she swept from the room like a ballerina exiting a stage.

The Prime Minister cringed with embarrassment.

"She's not as barmy as she seems," he explained. Then he thought about that for a moment. "Okay, she's *just* as barmy as she seems, but she really is the country's best language expert. It's just, she's fluent in so many languages she's forgotten which accent is hers."

At that moment, Mrs Du Monde swanned back into the room wearing a gold sari and a straw hat with corks hanging down from the rim.

"Mamma mia!" she cried, twirling a string of spaghetti above her head like a lasso. "Let's-a get on-a with-a translating the message-a, Billy. You shall-a tell me what-a you think-a they are saying, and I shall-a take-a some-a notes in-a my book."

BOOK, BOOK, BOOK, BOOK, BOOK, BOOK…

The word echoed inside my head like a gong had been struck in my brain, until suddenly it slipped from my mouth like a pickled-eel down a drainpipe.

"BOOK!" I yelled. And then, "BOOKS OF THE OLD TESTAMENT! Genesis! Exodus! Leviticus! Numbers! Deuteronomy! Joshua! Judges! Ruth! First

Samuel! Second Samuel!..."

"What is-a he-a doin'?" scowled Mrs Du Monde. "His-a brain is-a wonkier than-a the Leaning Tower of-a Pisa."

"Ezra! Nehemiah! Ester! Job!..."

"It's the Juice," said the Prime Minister. "He can't stop. Billy, try not to worry, you're nearly there, it'll soon be over."

"Micah! Nahum! Habakkuk! Zephaniah! Haggai! Zechariah! Malachi!"

GASP!

"Why has-a his face-a gone-a so red?" asked Mrs Du Monde. "Do you think-a he's-a gunna be sick?"

SICK, SICK, SICK, SICK, SICK, SICK…

Uh oh.

"SICK! WORDS THAT RHYME WITH SICK! Chick! Hick! Lick! Click! Flick! Slick! Nick! Snick! Pick! Quick! Rick! Brick! Crick! Trick! Tick! Stick! Thick! Wick!..."

"Oh no, Mrs Du Monde, you've started him off again!" wailed the Prime Minister.

"Broomstick! Sidekick! Picnic! Sceptic!..."

"Blimey, sport," said the woman, "I don't reckon you can blame this one on me. That kid's kangaroos are loose in 'is top paddock."

"Manic! Tannic! Stannic! Mechanic! Volcanic!

Organic! Titanic! Galvanic!..."

"Just ride it out, Billy," the Prime Minister urged. "There can't be an infinite number of words that rhyme with sick." He looked worriedly at Mrs Du Monde. "Can there?"

"Attic! Batik! Phatic! Static! Sciatic! Emphatic! Lymphatic! Pneumatic! Asthmatic! Erratic! Ecstatic! Antic! Mantic! Frantic! Pedantic! Gigantic! Atlantic! Romantic! Transatlantic! Megalithic! Allopathic! Chrematistic! Agonistic!"

GASP!

"Fair dinkum, that was bonzer, mate," the woman smiled. "What else can you—"

"Actually, Mrs Du Monde," the Prime Minister cut in, "would you mind staying quiet, just for the time being? I don't want you setting him off again."

"But the boy's on fire like a shrimp on a barbie," she said, "and I ain't heard nothing like it before, not in all the towns of Australia."

AUSTRALIA, AUSTRALIA, AUSTRALIA, AUSTRALIA, AUSTRALIA...

"Mrs Du Monde!" cried the Prime Minister. "What did I *just* say?!"

"AUSTRALIA! ALL THE TOWNS OF AUSTRALIA! Adaminaby! Paterson! Moulamein! Pallamallawa! Agnes Banks! Gundagai! Mount

Rivervie!..." The list went on and on and on (how many towns does one country *need?*) but this time, the more words I listed, the calmer I felt. The Prime Minister heard it in my voice. "Bullaburra. Glenbrook. Tarcutta. Yeoval…"

"Mrs Du Monde," he said, "Billy's taking charge of his brain again. The Juice must be reaching its peak. Quick, turn up the alien message."

"Inglewood. Warner. Roma. Stanthorpe…"

"Dotty as a dingo," she muttered, as the volume was raised. "Whacky as a wallaby. Potty as a possum."

"Katherine. Humpty Doo. Bulli. Springwood. Cardwell…"

"Louder, Mrs Du Monde, louder!"

"Bombala. Wellington. Wombarra. Richmond. Yungaburra…"

"Get ready… Here we go… Any second now…"

"Warrell Creek."

GASP!

"Now, Mrs Du Monde, now! Full volume, full volume!"

A button was pressed. The message blared out. And this time, the words made absolute sense.

"Billy Radcliffe," the alien said, "we have been waiting for you."

19

AUNTIE BRENDA

The Prime Minister saw the look on my face and signalled to a small microphone on the table in front of me.

"Billy," he said, "if you understand what the aliens are saying, you can talk to them through this. Just say whatever you feel is right," and he nodded seriously.

GULP!

Well, being able to speak Alien was weirder than finding a recipe for Auntie Brenda's Brain Booster Juice. It was weirder than becoming the headmaster of my own school. It was even weirder than Robert Williams being turned into a big ball of frogspawn.

But it was also weirdly awesome.

"Hello," I said nervously into the microphone. The words came out as a whistle, a kind of shrill noise with a bit of a warble. "Nice to meet you."

"The pleasure is mine," came the reply. It sounded like three voices, but it was actually one alien with *three mouths.* "I am waiting a long time to speak with you, Billy Radcliffe. It is many lightnesses ago that I come to your planet and leave a recipe in your worm corner."

"Wait, you mean...*you're* Auntie Brenda?"

There was a long silence, as if I had just asked the most difficult question in the whole universe.

"Erm, no," she replied. I could hear the confusion in her warble. "My name is Yan. I am a lifeform from another galaxy, speaking to you from the planet Jarghan. I stand outside your school gates when I visit your Earth and I leave milk in your Next-Door Shop. You are liking my fake humanoid skin, Billy Radcliffe, yes?"

"Oh, yes, it was very...rubbery."

"Thank you," she said, bashfully. "I want you to be having the recipe because my Future-Happenings Detector is saying there is a 99.9% chance that your boosted brain will be bringing you here, to the cellar of the basement at Number 10, Downing Street, London, England, Earth, The Milky Way, Space Zone B, Outer Universe, Star Code 417, where we can be talking on this basic inter-galactical communications device."

"You used science to predict the future," I said, my boosted brain understanding her perfectly. "But you could've spoken to me while you were here on

Earth. I wouldn't have minded."

The alien laughed.

"Billy Radcliffe, what will you be doing when an old human lady is ripping off her face in your Next-Door Shop and being an alien underneath?"

Her laughter was infectious and now I chuckled too.

"I'd probably scream," I admitted, "and then run away."

"Which is why I am boosting your brain and bringing you here," she replied, "where I can be telling you about an inter-galactical mission of great importance. Billy Radcliffe, my species are needing a human's help and our Best-Human-for-the-Mission Detector is choosing you."

"Me?!" I gasped. "But I'm not clever enough to tie my own shoelaces, let alone help with an inter-galactical mission. You should ask Mrs Du Monde or Professor Higgins. They'd be super-*super*-geniuses if they drank the Juice. Whereas I'm just, well, Billy."

There was a long pause.

"Billy Radcliffe," she said, "are you meaning these humans are better than you because they are clever?"

"Well, yes. The clever people get to sit at the Clever Table and nobody stamps on their feet.

Doesn't the same thing happen on your planet?"

"It does not, Billy Radcliffe. I come from a species of geniuses, but cleverness is not something we are achieving – it is something we are born with. It is no different to having green skin, or an extra tentacle, or being able to whistle through two mouths at once. No-one can be choosing what they are born with, Billy Radcliffe, and my species are not judging you on this."

"Your species sounds awesome," I told her.

"We are instead caring only about the choices you make," she went on. "For example, Billy Radcliffe, through my Super Long-Distance Goggles I am seeing you choose kindness with even the strangest of creatures."

"Oh, the worms aren't strange when you get to know them. They're just another species. It's no different to playing with a dog, or a cat, or an alien lifeform for that matter."

"You are correct, Billy Radcliffe. It is good to be mixing with those who are different to ourselves. But I am not meaning your long, slimy friends in the worm corner. I am meaning your friend who smells like a deceased creature of the ocean."

"Oh, *Colin,*" I said. "Yeah, Colin *is* a bit strange."

"And you are more bullied when you are with

him than when you are alone," the alien went on, "yet you are kind to him because you know how it feels to be without friends in a world full of humans. Billy Radcliffe, you are choosing kindness and our Best-Human-for-the-Mission Detector is choosing *you.*" Her words settled inside me like blossom and a warm feeling rose up to my face. "I shall be telling you now what the mission is, yes?"

I braced myself for the worst. What if she wanted me to navigate her spaceship through a blackhole? What if she wanted me to catch an evil human-munching Birdasaurus Pex with breath even smellier than Colin Bradley's? What if she wanted me to move to Mars and eat chocolate-coated caramel nougat for the rest of my life?

Actually, that last one didn't sound too bad.

"Your mission," she said, as if she was making the most important announcement of her life, "is to teach me your squiggly word symbols."

Silence.

Teach her my *what?*

"Erm, sorry," I said, "I don't understand."

"Your squiggly word symbols," she repeated, as if saying the words twice would explain them. "I make the Brain Booster recipe by copying your squiggly word symbols from the food packets in your

Next-Door Shop and you are looking at them to know the ingredients."

"Are you talking about—" There wasn't an Alien word for what I wanted to say, so I had to use the English word instead. "Are you talking about *writing?*"

"Writing," she repeated, whistling enthusiastically at this new language. "Yes, Billy Radcliffe, I am wanting to learn *writing*. Your squiggly word symbols are speaking without sound and lasting forever. But we do not have such a thing on our planet."

"You don't have writing?" I frowned. "But you're a species of geniuses. Why has no-one ever invented it?"

"We are geniuses of science," she said, "but no-one is being good at everything, Billy Radcliffe – your squiggly word symbols are going in one gill and out of the other for us. But if you are accepting your mission, I can be using what I learn to make *writing* for my own language."

My heart thumped at twice the speed. I couldn't believe what I was about to say.

"Well, I suppose if your detector thinks I'm the right human for the job," I said, "I could give it a go."

A shrill whistle of happiness rang out of the

speakers.

"Oh, Billy Radcliffe, this is wonderful!" squealed Yan with delight. "I think you are the kindest human and I am being right! You are making me the happiest lifeform this side of Space Zone G! But please, I must ask that you are keeping your mission a secret. When I am watching you through my Super Long-Distance Goggles, I am seeing some of your humans be cruel to each other. I do not wish to be splattered with sparkly lip-gloss or stapled to a wall when I am visiting your house, Billy Radcliffe."

"You want to come to my *house* for lessons?" I gasped.

"Yes, please," she replied. "Or, if you are preferring, you can be visiting my living-pod on the planet Jarghan, Middle Universe, Star Code 274."

"Thank you, but I think the bus fare to Star Code 274 is more than my pocket money can afford," I joked. The alien smiled. I could hear it in her whistle. "Yan," I said, hesitantly, "can I ask you a question? It's just, if *you're* not Auntie Brenda, who *is?*"

The alien gave a quizzical squeak.

"Billy Radcliffe, why do you keep asking if I am your parent's sister called Brenda?"

"Because it says Auntie Brenda's Brain Booster Juice at the top of the recipe. You wrote it there yourself."

There was a small snuffle and a sniff, followed by a raucous howl as the alien laughed her socks off (or whatever it is aliens wear on their feet).

"I am copying those squiggly word symbols from a food packet in your Next-Door Shop," she hooted, "because I am thinking they mean *bread*, not your parent's sister called Brenda. And I am writing them at the top of the page because bread is an important ingredient. Oh, I am such a silly extra-terrestrial lifeform!"

"Auntie Brenda's Medium Sliced Loaf," I breathed, remembering the bread from the Next-Door Shop. "But I didn't put any bread in the Brain Booster Juice and it still worked fine."

"This is because bread is not altering the effect of a potion. My species are using it to take away the terrible flavours of the less tasty foods." She snorted like a space-pig. "Fancy eating the eyes of a deceased ocean crustacean without any bread! You are fun, Billy Radcliffe." Just then, the speakers crackled. "The signal on your basic inter-galactical communications device is weakening," she said, hurriedly. "Billy Radcliffe, we must soon say good-bye."

"But wait, what shall I tell the Prime Minister

when he asks what we've talked about?"

"I am having a plan for this," she replied. "You can say we are talking about a new sustainable energy source I am discovering on your planet Earth. This way, we will be fooling your Prime Minister and also saving your planet from global warming. Now, let me be telling you what it is, Billy Radcliffe…"

And so, moments later, when the line dissolved and the alien had gone, I told the Prime Minister about the new sustainable energy source, just as Yan had suggested.

"Well, that's jolly nice of them to let us know," he remarked. "We'll never have to use any of those nasty fossil fuels ever again."

"That's right, sir," I said. "And remember, they won't be contacting us ever again so don't go looking for them. They were just passing and wanted to help us look after our planet before whizzing back off to their own. It's not like they're going to pop across the universe every Sunday to visit."

This was true – Yan was going to pop across the universe every *Monday* to visit.

"Well," the Prime Minister said, "we must act on their kind message by collecting as much of the new energy source as we possibly can. I'll appoint a New Energy Collection Minister as soon as I get back upstairs. Now, who shall I choose for the role?"

"Sir," I said, a lightbulb igniting over my head, "if you don't mind, I think I know just the person."

20

GOODBYE, MORAG

I was fastening my seatbelt in the back of the limousine outside Number 10, when somebody knocked on the window. It was Mrs Granger. She was sipping coffee from a cardboard cup and smirking happily.

"Barney No-Brain," she sneered, as I lowered the glass, "on your way back to the Wally Table, are you?"

"Yes, Mrs Granger, I'm afraid so."

"Best place for you," she scoffed. "Of course, *I'm* never setting foot in that classroom ever again. I've been hand-picked by the Prime Minister for a very important job. One that doesn't involve being plagued by imbeciles like you for the rest of my life. I'm going to be the New Energy Collection Minister."

"What an exciting opportunity, Mrs Granger. Good for you!"

The smile melted from her wrinkly old face (bullies hate it when their words bounce off you like rubber bullets) and she took a long swig of her coffee.

"Too right it's exciting," she said. "I'll be collecting a new sustainable energy source and saving the world. Whereas *you'll* be learning to tie your own shoelaces and picking your nose with the end of a pencil."

She fired those words at me like stones from a catapult, and missed.

"Our planet is lucky to have you, Mrs Granger. You really are a gift to humanity."

The ex-teacher crumpled the coffee cup in her fist, burning her hand on the contents.

"You can pretend not to care all you like, Barney No-Brain," she snarled, leaning in through the window, her chin-skin hanging over the glass like a deflated balloon, "but Morag Granger is headed for pastures new."

Morag?!

"How wonderful, Mrs Granger. I can see you now, skipping around in your new pasture, the autumn breeze blowing through your chin-hair as you scour the land for cow-pats."

"Ah," sighed the woman, wistfully, "like a young Julie An—" But then she stopped. "Cow-pats? What do you mean?"

"I mean poo, Mrs Granger."

"I know what a cow-pat is," she snapped, "but

why are you talking about them?"

"Because the new energy source comes out of a cow's bottom, Mrs Granger. Cow-pats. Big runny ones with steam coming off them, I shouldn't wonder."

"You're lying," she muttered, her chin-skin starting to wobble. "You're a horrible, nasty, little liar, Barney No-Brain."

"It's just a shame you can't turn down the job," I went on, "not now my boosted brain has told the Prime Minister what a marvellous idea it is. As far as he's concerned, you're the best poo-collector there is."

Her mouth puckered as the limousine-driver started the engine.

"The Prime Minister wouldn't listen to *you!*" she shrieked, trotting after the car as it pulled away from the kerb. "Nobody listens to *you!* You're stupid *Barney No-Brain!*"

That was it. Enough was enough.

"I am not!" I shouted back at her. "My name's Billy! Billy Radcliffe! And there's nothing wrong with *me,* Morag Granger, nothing at all!" and as we drove along Downing Street, the terrible teacher grew small in the distance until finally, *finally,* she was gone.

21

WORM BOOSTER JUICE

"Wotcha, Billy." Colin Bradley hung his coat on its peg and took a jar of rollmop herrings out of his pocket. "Are you still coming for tea later? Dad's making trout-head croutons to go with our soup."

The thought of fish faces floating on a sea of pureed crab-eyes drifted into my head.

"Of course," I told him. "Can't wait."

It was fun going to Colin's house. He showed me his tuna-tin collection and I showed him how to fold a Birdasaurus Pex, and when his dad dropped me home that evening, I thanked him for the lovely tea and waved good-bye with a smoked squid he'd let me take home for supper.

I found Andy in the living room, parading around like a peacock on a catwalk.

"All right, Billy boy?" he grinned, pushing his hair away from his eyes and turning up the collar of his denim jacket.

"Been out with Sarah?" I asked, casually.

"Yep," he replied, his cheeks turning pink. "She wrote me this wicked poem. Something about my head being a circle. I'm gunna write her one back," and he ran upstairs to his bedroom.

DING, DONG!

The doorbell sounded right on time and I answered it to a little old woman with a face like a porcelain doll.

"Hi," I whispered, beckoning her inside. "Mum's in the kitchen and Andy's in his room, so we won't be disturbed. Come on in," and closing the door, I ushered her quickly upstairs.

This was the fifth Monday Yan had visited. As usual she sat on the edge of my bed, reached into her coat pocket and pulled out a miniature bottle of Brain Booster Juice Concentrate. Then she took a pinhead-sized spoon and scooped up a tiny drop of the liquid.

Now, it's not usually a good idea to drink anything an alien lifeform offers you, no matter how small it is, but Yan and I were friends now. Plus, her version of the Juice tasted better than mine because she'd added bread to the recipe.

The moment it touched my tongue, my brain fired-up as if powered by rocket fuel.

"The door's closed," I told her, in fluent Alien. "You can take off your disguise now."

"Thank you, Billy Radcliffe," she said, and then, taking hold of her rubbery mask by the chin, she peeled it away from her face.

The first time Yan had removed her mask, I was terrified – she looked so different to anything I'd seen before. But now it was normal to see her three mouths, a pair of nostrils that opened and closed like gills, and a bald head with silvery skin that flashed metallic-green in the sunlight. In fact, I hardly noticed our differences at all.

Removing her human-gloves, Yan unfolded her twelve long fingers with a sigh of relief.

"Ah, that is feeling much better," she smiled. "But before we are starting our lesson, Billy Radcliffe, you must be having your gift."

"You don't need to bring me presents, Yan," I told her. "I like teaching you how to write."

The alien clicked her tongues and a small tub materialised on the bed.

"I know, Billy Radcliffe, but I am excited to be showing you what I am making this week. In this tub, you will be finding an exciting new formula. I am calling it Auntie Brenda's Worm Booster Juice."

"Wow, a potion to make Curly clever!" I exclaimed.

"Yes, Billy Radcliffe, it is for boosting your long

slimy friend's brain," she said, "but it is also for boosting his worminess," and I couldn't wait to try out my new potion at school the next day.

School was better now Mrs Granger had gone. Plus, Robert Williams had been sent to the Royal Academy for Compulsive Liars (which is what happens when you tell everyone the government turned you into frogspawn) and I wouldn't have to put up with Dana's mean words for much longer either.

"Oh *look,*" the girl smirked, the following morning, "Billy *Radcliffe's* playing with *worms* again."

"That's right," I said, carefully watching the ground where I'd sprinkled the Worm Booster Juice. I wasn't sure how a worm's worminess could be any wormier, but I was looking forward to finding out. "Don't you like worms, Dana?"

"Ew, *no,*" she snorted, "they're *gross* and they make my *skin* crawl. I don't know what's *worse,* hanging out with Colin the *Smelly* or hanging out with a bunch of *slimy,* muddy, horrible—"

But then she stopped. Dana Aintree stopped talking and she hasn't uttered a single word since. For at that very moment, Curly burst out of the ground in a fountain of dirt and the spiteful girl came nose-to-nose with the football-sized head of a twelve-foot worm.

The shock of it left her speechless forever.

"Marvellous," smiled Curly, looking *much* wormier than I'd ever seen him before. "Just marvellous."

And it really, *really* was.

Printed in Great Britain
by Amazon